Even if the Sky falls

Mia García

KATHERINE TEGEN BOOKS
An Imprint of HarperCollins Publishers

Katherine Tegen Books is an imprint of HarperCollins Publishers.

Even If the Sky Falls
Copyright © 2016 by HarperCollins Publishers
All rights reserved. Printed in the United States of America.
No part of this book may be used or reproduced in any
manner whatsoever without written permission except in the
case of brief quotations embodied in critical articles and reviews.
For information address HarperCollins Children's Books,
a division of HarperCollins Publishers, 195 Broadway,
New York, NY 10007.
www.epicreads.com

Library of Congress Control Number: 2016930032
ISBN 978-0-06-241180-8

16 17 18 19 20   CG/RRDH   10 9 8 7 6 5 4 3 2 1
❖
First Edition

For all those who kept me going

*"I love you the more in that I believe
you had liked me for my own sake
and for nothing else."*
—John Keats

*"Awake, dear heart, awake!
thou hast slept well; Awake!"*
—William Shakespeare, *The Tempest*

Heat of the Sun

STIFLING. CONFINING. SUFFOCATING. CHOKING. THE OPPOSITE of relaxing. Okay, I can do better with that last one.

But if I had to pick five adjectives to describe my past week in New Orleans, it would be those. Granted, they all mean the same thing, but they're all true—and technically, the opposite of what this trip is supposed to be. I believe what our church's youth coordinator promised my parents was a period of introspection and serenity seasoned with a dash of soul-searching, all wrapped in a tortilla of community outreach.

What I got was a week of hand-holding, spontaneous hugging, and people pretending they know just how I feel when they don't.

I cope by diving into my volunteer work, attempting to

nail together a wall or floor—I'm actually not sure which, but it's supposed to be flat—in this crazy heat and listening to the conversations of people—well-intentioned strangers, most of whose names I haven't bothered to learn—who are way too happy way too early in the morning. The chatter and the *thud, thud, thud* of my hammer against the wood form an odious melody, the kind that sinks under your skin and echoes long after you've tried to shake it. Before I know, I am drowning in it.

"'Fear no more the heat o' the sun, nor the furious winter's rages.'" For some reason, the words feel right as I let the hammer fall one more time, forcing the already secured nail farther down into the wood. "'Thou thy worldly task hast done, home art gone and ta'en thy wages.'"

"What?" a voice inquires behind me.

I turn to find Tavis staring at me, head turned to the side, examining me as if I were some odd creature. Considering I've been hammering down these planks of wood for the last hour like a madwoman, the wind tossing my hair every which way, a creature is probably what I look like.

"Nothing."

"Well, nothing sounded kinda weird." He smiles, running his fingers over his hair, damp with sweat, and just lingers . . . waiting for God knows what. I sigh, letting the heat sear me to a nice medium rare. He's closer than I'd like him to be—which is at least ten feet away at all times—but Tavis has a proximity issue.

2

I walk farther into my work area and away from Tavis—nice, cheerful, hovering Tavis, who is not entirely unpleasant but likes to drone on about . . . actually, I have no idea. I mostly space out when he's around. Still, Tavis believes he knows more about the world than I do, because he's nineteen and has been out of state or whatever. But even worse than his self-entitlement is that he's a hugger, a prolonged embrace sort of hugger that makes me feel like I'm promising something I never agreed to. He's also a "friend" of my brother, Adam, but not really. If I mentioned Tavis, Adam would probably have no idea who I was talking about.

Tavis is in charge of our ragtag group of . . . well, I guess you could call us a Christian Habitat for Humanity? Is Habitat already Christian? I don't know. I don't care. I'd needed a way out of . . . well, everything. So, when the opportunity presented itself to head out to New Orleans to help build houses for a couple of weeks, I jumped-slash-ran-slash-practically threw myself at the chance. But if I have to answer "Isn't it a beautiful day?" as sweat stains become a permanent addition to my wardrobe one more time I might just . . . just what?

I count to ten.

Tavis doesn't get the hint that I'm not interested. Though nowadays I'm not much interested in anything.

When I look back, Tavis is inspecting me, and a shiver travels up my spine—I hope he doesn't try to continue our earlier "let's talk about our feelings" conversation. He does. I feel him inch closer to me as his questions get more and more detailed.

"But truly, Julie, have you even talked about it since it happened?" The heat from his skin is more stifling than the sun. It closes the world around me, walling me in.

"Maybe it will help to imagine yourself on that road. What if you'd been behind the wheel?" His hand reaches toward mine. "In a way do you feel like you were behind the wheel?" I bend down to pick up a saw, a move I hope seems casual, before I realize it's a mistake. Tavis squats down beside me, and I feel his fingers graze my skin. I stand, brushing the hair off my face.

"I've got to go meet my team." My eyes dance around the half-built frame of a tiny house: all bones and angles, on the cusp of becoming something of value. "Um, Nancy is waiting for me to go over . . . hammering techniques."

"I'm not sure I know a Nancy."

"Really?" I shrug. "She loves you. You and Nancy should elope."

I flee to the other side of the construction site.

I stare up at the sun, back out after disappearing behind the clouds, letting the bright rays pierce my vision. Despite the constant gusts and the promise of rain later in the day, the heat is palpable, and for a moment I let the burning sink deeper and deeper. Hell, I forgot the sun could be so . . . violent.

"Jules?"

I bristle. No one but my brother and friends call me Jules. No one. Especially not Tavis.

"Julie?"

"It's from *Cymbeline*."

"What?"

"What I was saying before. It's a quote. From *Cymbeline . . .*"

Blank stare.

"You know, Shakespeare? I performed it one summer in my drama class. It's about death and how once you're dead you don't really have to worry about anything anymore. Not the heat of the sun or anything. You know?"

Pitying smile. I turn away and stumble into more smiles and soft eyes that ask whether or not I need a hug. Goddammit.

"Never mind." I wipe the sweat off my brow. "Just popped into my head while I was thinking of the heat."

"Yeah." Tavis covers his eyes with his hand as he peers at me again. "Louisiana heat is no joke."

He tosses a cool water bottle my way.

"Don't forget to stay hydrated, right?"

"Right!" I say too cheerfully because Tavis is nineteen and a multistate traveler.

I know he has more to say—he always does—each breath he takes is in expectation of something, and I can't shake the feeling that the something is me.

The great Escape

I CASUALLY WALK A WAYS AWAY FROM HIM AND DOWN THE bottle in less than a minute, ignoring the bit of my brain that says I am probably dehydrated, because that part has clearly not gotten the memo about not agreeing with anything Tavis has to say. When I look over I notice that he hasn't taken his eyes off me and suddenly, despite the distance, I feel trapped. He smiles when I notice him and I let the corners of my mouth lift just a bit before turning to toss the bottle away in the makeshift recycle bin we put together.

"Time for prayer circle," he says to me.

Great. Prayer circle is usually at the end of the day, but we're cutting work short today for some reason or other.

There might be a storm coming, but I wasn't really listening when he was talking about it. All I know is he'll probably want to hold my hand.

"I'll be there in a second." I wait until he's far enough away before I wipe my brow with the bottom of my shirt. This heat and humidity is going to kill me, if not from dehydration (so, *so* much sweating), then by burning me to a crisp. The sun has been in and out for most of the day, but I can still feel it even when it's hidden behind the clouds. It's been too long since I've been in heat like this. Abuela Julia would be disappointed by my lack of stamina.

But it's not just the heat now that's building. I've tried ignoring it all day, concentrating on the tasks at hand, but it's still there. Between Tavis, the looks, the impromptu chats, the sweating, hand-holding, and incessant sharing of feelings—

Has the sun always been this hot? I feel something about to bubble up from inside me. I am an animal in a zoo and everyone is watching, waiting for me to perform, to cry, to break down, to let them help me. Save me. That's what I should want, right? Help. Pity. Absolution.

"Anytime, Julie. Anytime."

"How about next Tuesday?"

The reply leaves my lips before I can stop myself. Old Julie would never have snapped back; she would've apologized and rushed over. She was the type of girl who stayed late painting fake moss on rocks for a community production of *Joseph and the Amazing Technicolor Dreamcoat*. New Julie still smiles, but it never reaches her eyes. She finds excuses not to hang out with her friends and avoids eye contact. New Julie just wants to make everything go away. New Julie doesn't want to be Julie anymore. *And how exactly do you do that?*

As I trudge my way over, I notice another group—on their last day—packing up to head out into the city to celebrate all the good they've done on their project. I wonder if they can feel the need and desperation radiating out of me. Probably not. Tavis motions to the girl beside him, making a place for me in the prayer circle; I sigh and lock hands with him—his hands are moist yet rough, his grip weak yet stifling. Our heads bow in prayer.

"Dear Heavenly Father," he starts.

The sweat works its way down my back, one rivulet after the other. I curse every single fashion decision I made this morning. Shirt? Too hot. Jeans? Clearly invented by a demon spawn from hell. The wind picks up a little but not enough to dampen this heat. Tavis gives my hand a little squeeze as I start to squirm.

HEEL, Tavis.

A laugh escapes, but I hide it with a cough. *Don't let anyone see cracks in the walls, Jules.* People don't like to see them. Not the true cracks that travel deep and splinter your heart. The ugly cracks that aren't easily healed. Those you keep to yourself.

I push the thoughts back deep into my mind and concentrate on the pinpricks that travel up and down my arms. Everything is closing in on me. Fabric too close to my skin, Tavis's hand too hot in mine, the sun, the sweat, the lack of wind. My kingdom for some precipitation!

Katie, Katherine? No, Katie is to the other side of me and gives me a quick reassuring smile like she for sure knows I'm about to lose it but could I please keep it together for Jesus this one time?

Another laugh.

Jesus, Jules, keep it together for Katie!

I take a deep breath and with it comes Adam again, images of closed doors and red-rimmed eyes and hush-toned conversations.

This is all a mistake. I should be home with Adam, not stuck here pretending this work is of any help. I look around. Everyone's head is bowed, their bodies serene, as Tavis continues to pray for every single person in the world, for understanding of what the Lord's plan is for us all.

There is no plan. I see this now. Not God's plan anyway.

Behind us the other group is filing into a tiny bus that belongs in a commercial for coconut rum, their voices a cacophony of joy, ready to head somewhere fabulous on their journey of awesome while I'm caught in the grip of Tavis's clamminess. My body leans toward them, sensing a way out.

I feel Tavis's grip tighten, trying to bring me back to where I belong . . . where he wants me to belong. But my body takes over. I pull away, forcing a cough and excusing myself with a few quick hand gestures. Tavis continues praying as I maneuver over to the small transport van where we keep all our stuff. I feel more in control than I have in weeks as I grab my purse, tuck in another bottle of water, and then slip behind the super-happy group heading out of the Ninth Ward. I keep my head down, and no one stops me as I board the rum bus all the way to the back.

When the engine starts up I expect to be caught at any moment, for someone to scream, "Hey, you with the scowl! You aren't part of the super-shiny-group-of-happiness. Get out of here before you infect us all!" But I'm not. As we head out, I inch closer to the window and hunch down in my seat.

I listen to them jabber on about what things they want to see and what they want to eat and take pictures of, and I am lulled into a sense of accomplishment, of freedom. I watch the stream of houses as they pass by: Damaged. Rebuilt. Rebuilt. Damaged. Destroyed. Destroyed. Empty lot. The aftermath of almost a decade of storms. Some homes were easier than others to fix: water damage, missing roof. Others had been torn down and built back up on stilts. They remind me a bit of the houses by the beaches in Puerto Rico that I saw when I used to visit with my grandmother, the color of guava, mangoes, and avocados.

Brightened even more with touches of white, colors defiant against the past. It wasn't just Katrina either, I learned that from the locals who drove us down to the work site each day. Nature didn't stop after that hurricane. Nature kept coming, kept destroying. It didn't stop, but neither did New Orleans. The city picked itself up; its heart kept beating.

I zone out trying to find a pattern to the growth and destruction. A tingle in my stomach starts. Chatter bubbles up again, like a pot of water ready to boil over with excitement. We're almost there. Where? I have no idea, but we're close.

Until we're not, and the bus stops. I jump up from my seat, looking out the window for any clue of what's going on—all I see around me are tall buildings, mostly fancy hotels from the looks of it. My fellow travelers are as clueless as I am, though their heartbeats probably aren't as steadily on the rise as mine. My mind races with possibilities: We've run out of gas or coconut rum, or lost a spark plug or the carburetor is broken or Tavis has caught up to us, running all the way here, desperate to hold my hand in his clammy palm once again. The driver ushers everyone out—whatever stopped the bus has stopped the AC and the temp is ticking its way up to sticky and sweaty quite fast.

I step out of the bus and pretend to head over to everyone else, but instead I round a corner and keep going. I take a chance that no one will notice the girl that isn't supposed to be there. I'm right. No one runs after me or yells my name as I sprint away. When I finally find a street sign I know I'm somewhere on Canal Street—which means nothing to me, but should the police put on a dramatic chase for my return, I can answer without impunity when questioned that "Yes, sir, I was on Canal Street."

Keeping a brisk pace, I walk a straight path through the neighborhood, paved roads turning into cobblestones, veering left away from the hotels and into the zone of smaller buildings. I don't register which direction I'm going, just that I need to keep going until I feel—until I know—that I am as far away from the group, from Tavis, as possible.

A strange lightness takes over my body the farther and farther I get from our construction site. Perhaps delirium or heatstroke has finally set in because my legs don't burn or ache, but I keep pushing my body forward to freedom.

When I finally slow down I realize: 1. I have no idea where I am (as I am no longer on Canal Street), and 2. Everything is gorgeous. I mean seriously gorgeous. The buildings, the terraces, the dangling flowers all over the houses, like *whoa*. I spot an entrance in one of the brick buildings leading to a wide-open courtyard—a perfect place to stop for a moment and gather myself. I walk in, pass some signs that declare it the Jean Lafitte Visitors Center, and collapse on the nearest bench. It's quiet here and cool in the shade with the occasional breeze flowing in, making it even more of a tiny oasis.

Done singing its song of escape, my heart finally quiets

down, drifting into its regular beat of life, and I don't know if it's the feel of the breeze traveling along my skin or the tranquil sounds of bubbling water that do it, but before I know it a laugh erupts, then another. Because I did it! I'm friggin' free! Sure, I don't know where I am (minor setback) and I'm probably being tracked as we speak (future major setback) but I'm free. Only *I* can decide what to do next, not Tavis, not my parents, not Adam. Me.

Go, me.

Do Whatever a Grown Man in a Tutu Tells You

Pulling the water bottle out of my purse, I swig about half of it before tucking it back in. A quick look at my phone puts me in the French Quarter, which explains the gorgeous architecture with its delicate iron balconies shaped into *fleurs-de-lis* and other looping forms. Even the small courtyard I've escaped to is breathtaking. The central fountain is tiny, nestled among various trees and potted plants; it feels like the sort of place where time is relative, a minute turning into an hour into a day, and a dangerous place to set goals. Tavis promised us a guided tour of the Quarter a few days ago but never delivered. Good ol' Tavis.

There's a burst of laughter to my left, and a group of girls run out of what has to be a hidden public restroom. I say a prayer that it is at least semi-clean and head inside where I take one look at myself and immediately scrub my face with the hand soap. It's impressive how easily dirt can cling to your skin, shirt, hair. After redoing my ponytail, I pull my backup tank and deodorant from my bag—just because I can't smell the stink doesn't mean other people won't.

Using the dirty shirt to rid myself of the last of the sweat, I pull the new tank on and head out the door, back to my freedom.

I follow the beat of my heart down one street after another, not knowing how long I've walked, until I realize it's not my heart I'm hearing, it's music.

The beat of drums and cymbals and trombones travels up my legs and sinks into my skin as if I were the instrument itself; the beat moves forward and I move with it, weaving through the streets until I'm deep in the current of this magical, writhing mass. All around me bands of fairies, demons, and leprechauns head down the streets, inviting me into their revelry. I twist around, capturing every single amazing flash of color—blues, fuchsias, yellows—and it takes a moment to identify them as people.

What is this? I wonder when I bump straight into a fish wearing a tutu.

Not really a fish—obviously—but a man around my father's age, his brown skin dusted with powdered gold, a vibrant pattern of blue and green scales painted all over his arms and legs, and on top of his head a coral-shaped crown made of aluminum foil and spray-painted gold. A snort quickly escapes as I imagine my quiet-as-a-mouse dad wearing a tutu and fairy dust.

"What you laughing at, girl?" the man shouts with the brightest smile I've seen in ages. I can't help but smile back at him—he's contagious.

"You look AWESOME!"

He tips an imaginary hat. "Thank you, child. Takes a village." Looking up at me, he drops his smile. "But where's your costume? Don't tell me your village was out today!"

He laughs at his own joke, like my dad would, which I usually never find funny but for some reason is very charming whilst wearing a tutu.

"I—don't actually know what's going on right now," I yell over the blasts of the horns. The music seems to be coming from every balcony, every corner, every plank of wood. New Orleans is made of music, and I am right in the thick of it.

"What you mean you don't know? You in New Orleans and you don't know it's Mid-Summer Mardi Gras, girl?"

I shake my head. "Guess not."

"Well"—he pauses for effect—"it's Mid-Summer Mardi Gras, girl! One of the biggest celebrations of the year—and my favorite. You in luck." His many-layered tutu sways with his hips. "And so is everybody here, especially me!" His laugh travels up, up into the beat. "We're all heading up to the Maple Leaf for the parade if you want to come with. You better do something about your costume, though. Shows a lack of imagination walking around like that—plus it hurts my heart. And nobody hurts my heart, young lady, not even a pretty little thing like you."

With a flick of his hands he shoos me away. "Go on now. The next time I see you, you better sparkle."

"Sparkle?"

"Um-hmm." He waves as he travels into the throng. "All that glitters! Don't break ol' Julius's heart!"

"Julius?"

He nods. "Like the caesar."

"How do I get to the Maple Leaf?"

Julius turns with a swish of his skirt. "You can walk for an hour, or take the streetcar, or you can scoot onto that van over there." He points to a van painted just as bright as the people around it. "Don't keep Mid-Summer waiting!" And with a wink he is gone, swallowed into the pulsing heart of the city.

Pushing my way against the crowd is harder than I anticipate—how do salmon do this? But then I spot a grocery on the corner and dive in. The cool air and fluorescent light have a calming effect I wasn't expecting. I walk through the aisles unsure of what I'm looking for when it hits me.

I snag a roll of red cellophane, two wire hangers, and some clear tape.

"Do you mind if I stand over here and take all this stuff apart?" I ask the lady behind the counter after I pay.

She looks at me for a while. "Nah, guess not."

I break into the hangers first, reshaping them until they look somewhat like butterfly wings. Then I wrap them in the red cellophane, probably left over from a Valentine's Day promotion or something. When I'm done I secure them to my back with bits of tape. They promptly fall down. On my third try I'm ready to give up.

"You need extra support," the clerk says. I guess she'd been watching me all along. "Hold on." She picks up her purse from under the register and moves stuff around, pulling a pair of heels, a dress, and a million other things from her bag. She is maybe twenty-five? Twenty-three? Her bleach-blond hair and hazel eyes spark with amusement as she finally excavates a few large safety pins. "Here you go; this might help."

"Thanks!"

After another failed attempt at putting wings on myself, the clerk snatches them out of my hands and motions me to turn around. "I'm going to pin these to the back of your bra—is that all right?" I nod and she pins away.

"Can I ask you a quick question?" I say.

"Mm-hmm."

"That, like, random van taking people to the Maple Leaf out there? Is that legit or should I be worried?"

She muffles a laugh. "Legit. The OAK Krewe sometimes

helps coordinate them—they put on Mid-Summer. Helps with the traffic and all."

"Awesome, thanks!"

When she's done I wiggle from side to side, testing the strength of my new wings.

"Not bad," she says. "You're missing something though." She digs back into the purse and pulls out gold-hued eye shadow and what I think is body glitter. "Um-hmm. All that glitters, come here."

"Oh, it's okay. I don't really—"

"All that glitters," she repeats, a bit annoyed now.

"I'm sorry . . . I don't."

"It's this year's theme. All that glitters or glistens, shines, or whatever it is."

"That doesn't really mean . . . ," I reply.

She waves me off. "I know what it means, don't get hung up on it." She motions me forward. "Plus every now and then you need a little something in your life—something that shines so bright it pushes everything else away. Right?"

Her words echo. Something that shines so bright it pushes everything else away. It's just what I need.

"Come on now." Her patience is running low, and I step forward.

"Do you always carry all of that in your bag?"

Smiling, she tells me to close my eyes. "I do if it's Mid-Summer. Store closes in about an hour, but the party is just starting! You think I can make it home to change with this crowd? No way—gotta be prepared. Got myself a nice mermaid costume tucked in the back. My skin's already itching to put it on and head out."

"Well, I bet you'll look amazing."

"Oh I will," she says with a smile. Satisfied with her work, she sends me off and motions to the person behind me. "Next!"

I exit the store transformed with wings on my back and glittery—no, sparkly—skin ready for Mid-Summer. The van ride takes no more than ten to fifteen minutes—it's all a blur of bumping into other fairies, tangled wings, and mermaids who share the same electricity, the same anticipation, as we near our destination. We flow out of the van like memories caught on a slow shutter speed: bursts of energy rushing into the world.

I disappear into the crowd, dancing with strangers, alive, free, and for the first time in a very long time, I don't think of Adam.

WHAT FOOLS THESE *mortals be!* I think as I travel from block to block. The party is endless and unstoppable. When the wind coils around us we twirl, letting it pick up our skirts, ready for a dance. Every corner, every alley is infected with music, dance, and sweat as we all parade down the street as one big entity. Ahead of me I see a sun, dripping glitter as it's pulled along by a motorcycle, while behind me someone has recreated a chunk of the ocean floor out of pipes and streamers. I can't help but be disappointed in the few who haven't bothered to dress up. I shake my head, channeling Julius, although by the end of the night they will shine with us all.

I catch a glimpse of a tutu and I run, sure I've caught up with Julius, ready to show off my wings and my sparkle, but I end up being sorely mistaken as the man I approach is not only not Julius, but his costume and attitude lack Julius's lively imagination. I am not impressed, and he is not amused.

I don't let it stop me; the rhythm carries me from one block to another. I follow brass bands, dance with strangers both young and old to music I've never listened to. It is loud and fast but lacks the shallowness of most dance music, like it has a soul, a story. Quick but not repetitive, each swell takes turns I am unfamiliar with; the type of music you can't overthink. For a moment I close my eyes. I want to let go and dance until my body breaks away into hundreds of little notes, floating above the crowd until I disappear. Truly free.

I bump up against a tall, broad-shouldered stranger, a deep smell of whiskey surrounding him like a cloud. I crinkle my nose as I turn to apologize. Then I freeze. He looks just like Adam.

In Hindsight

I LOVED MY BROTHER, ADAM—NO . . . NO. I LOVE MY BROTHER, Adam—I have to stop doing that, I really do. It's the anger talking and screaming and doing most of the thinking. Oh yeah, and the guilt. Anger and guilt are what drive this ship these days mostly—but they weren't important, not back then, not in the time before everything happened. Now it seems like anger and guilt are all I have left, anchors during this screwed-up situation that I never thought I'd be in. But that's the now. Back then I was happy. I went to church. I smiled all the friggin' time and ate without my mom having to yell at me. I didn't snap at my friends or refuse to see them or refuse to talk to anyone for days. . . .

More important, back then I was just a girl who missed her brother. My amazing, strong, older brother who made the perfect Sunday pancake; who knew just what scary story to tell me so I couldn't sleep a wink at night; who knew when I needed him to defend me at school and when I could handle things on my own; who knew I needed to share a laugh or roll my eyes at our parents when they acted ridiculous; and who went off to war to do his duty and left me behind.

Despite how proud we all were of my brother, I missed him terribly—as did our parents, of course—there wasn't a Sunday Mass where we didn't pray for his safe return and the return of all the other soldiers out there. "What kind of people would we be if we only prayed for our own family?" my mom would say. I never answered. I didn't—and still don't—understand why it's selfish to pray just for the ones you love. I smiled and joined my mother in a prayer for every soldier in the world and their families, but silently, in my own heart and mind, I only prayed for Adam.

It had been almost a year since he'd been gone—his gnawing absence a wound that was scabbed over and picked on occasion to reveal the pulsing pain of loss. Was he okay? Did he think of us? What did he do every day? Did he . . . kill people? Would God forgive him if he did? Would I?

We went on with our days, my parents pretending to

care about what I did, hanging out with friends, having fun, only to have the guilt bombard me at night, keeping me up, until exhaustion won.

Also, funny thing, when someone you love goes off to war, it's like you aren't allowed to say how much you miss them, at least not to other people. Well, you *are*, but you have to then agree that he's doing the right thing and fighting for his country and missing him becomes this childlike statement that gets swept under the rug, like "I'm bored" or "Are we there yet?"

I'd encountered this phenomenon more than once in the year he was gone and most always from an adult asking me how we were holding up and how my parents were. "I miss Adam," I would always say, and they'd nod and tell me all the good he was doing overseas as if it couldn't get done by anyone else, and aren't you just being a bit selfish, young lady? At least that's what it felt like.

Then they'd smile that sad, pitying smile and pat me on the cheek, and I would make a note not to talk to anyone about Adam.

I missed my damn brother. Let that be that.

By then the emails had stopped between us—he simply didn't have the time to write back, my parents insisted. But I kept going—I kept writing—almost as if to spite everyone, I didn't care if he read them or not, I needed to write to him, to tell him about my day and who said what stupid thing in class and wasn't it just ridiculous that such and such happened. I imagined Adam poring over my words, remembering what it was like to be back home surrounded by those he loved and maybe those he hated, clinging to the normal in any way he could.

A year after he was deployed we got word my brother was coming home. We were beyond excited—we cleaned and scrubbed every single surface of the house, bought all of his favorite snacks despite my mom's opinion on what the Lord thinks of sugar. We fixed his room till it was so perfect it hid all our worries.

When he walked into the house, I leaped into his arms, crying and saying how happy I was that he was home. He patted me on the head—"Me too, kid, me too"—and hugged our parents. He excused himself and passed out on his bed. That was fine, of course, he was tired; he'd just come back from a war and needed rest. We ate dinner and had dessert without him. We left him a serving in the microwave in case he woke up in the middle of the night.

We did this for one week straight. I'd wake up in the morning and Adam would be asleep in his room, and he'd still be there by the time I got back from school. We didn't pressure him—he needed time, my parents said. We didn't know what he'd been through, and it was best not to pressure him into doing anything he didn't want to. Lots of people weren't lucky enough to get their loved ones back.

But I was impatient. I stayed up late and watched his door until my eyes burned, only to fall asleep and wake tucked into my own bed. I knew it was Adam who carried me to my room; my father's had a bad back for most of his life—he can only manage a good-sized book and that's it. I kept on watching, hoping I would catch him eventually.

I did. One night I woke up snuggled into my bed when I heard the scuffle of plates and ran down to the kitchen to join him. He slammed the microwave shut, pressing the buttons as hard as he could.

"Gee—trying to wake up the whole house?" I said, hoping he'd heard the lightheartedness in my voice. Adam and I were finally awake at the same time; we could finally talk or not talk and just sit in the same room together, which was totally fine, as long as he let me stay. I said a silent prayer that he would.

"Sorry, kid."

"S'okay." I sat down by the kitchen table and watched him scrambling for utensils, then searching for a glass, and finally pulling out Dad's secret stash of whiskey, which wasn't really a secret. He kept it at the back of one of the cabinets in plain view and took it out to mark special occasions. I'd only seen him crack it when Adam graduated college, and I'm sure he would've opened it again at Adam's arrival if he'd been awake at all this last week.

"That's for special occasions," I said because I'm such a Goody Two-shoes and I was worried. But now, in hindsight, I think I could see it, feel it in the pauses and stilted conversation, in the cautiousness I felt when approaching him, like he would break and shatter into something sharp.

If I'd only known how little my brother was holding it together, how large the cracks were.

Adam poured enough to fill half the glass, then looked up at me. "I'll tell you a little secret I learned while I was deployed, kiddo. Every day you're alive is a special occasion."

He downed the whiskey in two swigs, and for the first time since he'd gotten home, Adam smiled.

So I smiled back.

The Midsummer Boys

THE SOUNDS OF MID-SUMMER HAVE DISAPPEARED IF ONLY FOR a moment, paused, waiting for my mind to catch up to my heart.

It's just me and the whiskey breath of this stranger, Adam's twin, leaning toward me.

"Sorry." I recover and try to compose myself, but I lose my rhythm and stumble to the ground. The Adam look-alike tries to reach for me, but I wave him away along with the memory of Adam. He shrugs and continues on, leaving me on the ground as the party goes on around me. I am a rock in the flow of a river. It parts but doesn't stop.

"You okay, honey?"

I turn my head and look up into a lovely set of brown

eyes and a warm smile. A woman of about eighty extends her hand to me, lifting me up. There's no trace of the Adam look-alike, and I shake off the thought that it was in any way a sign that I should be back with the group. I smile up at my helper.

"Yes, thank you. Just lost my place."

"Well, it's right here." She motions me to follow her back into the mass, and I do. "You don't want to miss the Midsummer Boys!"

"The what?"

She's dancing away from me, and I marvel at her stamina. I'm shaking my head, back into the sway, watching this woman who could be my grandmother shimmy with more energy than I've ever had, when I see him. I mean, I see the whole street band tucked in front of one of the many stores down the block, momentarily stationary, but I only *really* see him.

I stop staring, because I was—am—staring, and try to focus on anything else. The balconies, the half-naked ladies in costume—some just half naked; I mean, more power to them—but still I keep drifting back to him, a tall, muscular boy with a 'fro dyed electric blue and a cardboard top hat with big paper donkey ears poking out of its side. He sways back and forth to the music, his smile so wide it takes over his face. I am caught, frozen, as the parade continues to flow. I smile before I can stop myself, and our eyes lock.

For a moment I think I know him. His smile, his eyes,

something feels familiar, but I would remember if we had met.

He's singing something, but I can't hear the words. His gaze is locked on mine and that's all there is.

Oh yeah, I would remember that smile.

Look away, Jules! Look away!

But I can't. I'm stuck in the tractor beam of his eyes and lips. I've never wanted to touch a guy's lips as much as I do now. I turn, expecting to find his gorgeous bohemian girlfriend right behind me and instead see my eighty-year-old savior dancing up a storm. Maybe he is smiling at her? Because who wouldn't? She's fantastic! I turn back and . . . he's definitely looking at me. "Fairy girl!"

Annnnnnd he is calling me over.

Crap.

"Fairy girl!" he shouts again, this time motioning me over with his banjo—did I forget to mention the banjo? He has a banjo. And lean, long fingers that strum said banjo like no banjo has ever been strummed before. "Fairy girl!"

He could mean anyone really. Half the people here have wings.

"Red-winged fairy girl, I see you!"

Maybe not.

I move closer, weaving through people, careful not to snag my wings on the way. "Hello," I say once I'm close enough to hear him without having to shout.

Hello?

Why didn't I say "Hi"? Don't look so eager, Jules.

"Hello back." He smiles and continues to play, accompanying the band. "I like your wings!"

"Thanks. I made them myself, like, an hour ago. I like your hat."

"Thank you. Took me days."

We smile at each other like idiots. Or at least I do. Yeah, probably just me on the idiot front.

When he turns away, I look him up and down, taking in his hands as they strum along, his chest (he has a few buttons of his shirt unbuttoned, so sue me—I ogled him), a thin gold band around his left wrist, blue-tipped hair and handmade hat with the ears. A grin spreads across my face. "'What fools these mortals be,'" I say again, and he looks back to me, beaming.

"You're Bottom, right? From *A Midsummer Night's Dream*?"

He bows and brays like a donkey.

I take in the rest of his band, dressed in a similar style, when it hits me. "You're the Midsummer Boys!"

"That we are. You a fan?"

"I—uh."

Crap, say yes!

He laughs. "No worries. No one really knows us; I'm just messing with you."

"I love the name though."

"Nice, isn't it? Just thought of it today! Last week we

were No Return Policy." He shrugs. "I like the Midsummer Boys better though, don't you?"

I nod.

"Let's do 'I am that merry wanderer of the night,'" he says to the guys behind him, and the boys start the tune. He turns back to me. "Will's got a way with words, don't you think, Sunshine?"

With a wink he dives into the song, joining a buzok (I kid you not, I've never even heard one being played live; it looks like someone whittled down the top half of a guitar's body and left the bottom as is), a fiddle, and an accordion. I am entranced by his fingers and try to look away, but only find my way back to his smile. He knows this I think because he can't stop grinning. My cheeks flush, and I decide to give in to the music and try my hardest to forget about the Electric Blue Boy who knows the effect he has on women. I only catch a few of the lyrics that say "a night to wake, a night to live," and I gather these words to me and take them with me through the night.

The band finishes "The Merry Wanderer" and picks up another—the crowd cheering as they do. It's Mid-Summer, and no one likes a lull. Shaking my hips from side to side, I find the rhythm of one song after another. Electric Blue Boy follows me with his eyes, and that's all I need to join in on the fun.

I shimmy over to the nearest café and borrow a pair of spoons, slapping them together across my thigh to try them out. They make a nice, crisp sound that rings clear even through the pulse of the French Quarter. I have no idea who this new Julie is, but she feels fantastic and I let her take over. Electric Blue watches me, eyebrows arched up in surprise.

"You going to join us, Sunshine?"

I strike the spoons against my thigh. "Keep up if you can!"

I have no idea what I'm doing, but I don't care. I probably sound terrible but somehow it all works out. Our arms rub against each other, I feel a lightness I'm not expecting, and I hope it happens again as the crowds press us nearer and nearer. He leads the way down the street, pushing his shoulder against mine, and we walk that way for a song or two. Or three? I feel . . . I don't know what I feel, it's different and new and I can't describe it, and as I look up into the sky, I catch a glimpse of the quarter moon, peeking out from behind the clouds, pushing away the pitiful sun, ready to take over.

"Come on, Sunshine," he says over his shoulder.

The accordion player is leading a line of revelers out of our secluded little corner and back into the mass. I follow. The wind follows, moving my wings back and forth—I'm flying. Street after street I play my little spoons until my arms hurt.

Eventually we stop and the crowds clap as the Midsummer Boys take a bow and the crowds rejoin the living, pulsing mass that is the Mid-Summer mayhem.

My phone buzzes, a quick look tells me it's Tavis: Where are you? I drop the spoons, quickly lost in a sea of legs. There are twenty messages on my phone from Tavis. How did I not notice this? They're all variations of the same question: Where are you? We're worried about you. Everyone is out looking for you. I scan the crowd, hiding my growing panic, but don't see him.

You're just being paranoid, Jules. No way he can find you here.

"Take a bow, Sunshine." Electric Blue Boy looks back, reaching for me.

We lace hands; the strength in his grip feels comforting, reassuring, and surprisingly intimate. Does anyone else notice how my gaze drifts down to our hands entwined? Do they share the flush across my skin? We bow to what's left of the crowd.

"It's over?" I manage, gripping the phone tighter. It's still buzzing, pulling me away from Electric Blue's touch, and his steady pulse that seems to sync with mine.

"This is just the pre-party. Parade starts at eight—still a couple of hours to kill before then, plus gotta scope out a place to take it all in." He takes his hat off to slide the banjo across his back before replacing it with a flourish. "You?"

I ignore the buzzing and focus on his eyes, shoving the phone back in my pocket.

Before I can answer, his three bandmates huddle

around us. "Sunshine, these are the boys: Domínguez on the accordion, Taj on the buzok, and Danny on the fiddle. Otherwise known as my backup."

I nod, ready to wave and disappear into the crowd. I've never been good with group conversations, feeling most comfortable hanging out in a corner with my closest friends, Kara or Em. Suddenly, Danny, who is tall and stocky with a tailored vest and hat, pushes Electric Blue to the side and shakes my hand. "Pleasure."

Each of the boys follows suit, and before I know it I feel at ease.

"So you got someplace to be, Sunshine?" Electric Blue asks me.

My phone buzzes in my pocket, I pull it out halfway. Crap. Another message from Tavis, then my parents, Em— who called her?—and a couple from Adam. *Shit.*

When I look up the boys are all waiting for me.

What's it going to be, Julie? You've come this far.

I scroll through the messages one last time, then I shut the phone off and shove it deep into my bag.

"Not really."

Electric Blue smiles, and I think maybe I should call *him* Sunshine. He bows and asks for my hand, which I give. He loops it around his arm and says, "Well, you do now."

What's in a name?

IT IS CROWDED AS HELL ON OAK STREET AS I NAVIGATE THE throngs, gripping Electric Blue's hand. I should probably feel self-conscious about holding hands with a boy I just met, but the alternative would be getting lost in the sea of nymphs and jesters and the vibration of the city, a beat that practically lifts me off my feet. Plus his hand feels welcome in mine, and I hope he never lets go.

He smiles back at me as we find a semi-quiet corner where we can finally rest. We lean against the wall of the building and survey the mass of dancers before us, trying not to look at each other too much.

He smells a bit like vanilla mixed with sweat, and how did the word "delicious" just pop into my mind?

I pray he thinks the now-permanent flush across my cheeks is due to the heat and not our proximity to each other.

"You okay?" He leans into me, and I feel his breath on my cheek.

"Yeah." I rub my forearms. "Just a bit overwhelmed."

About this, about life, about everything. I just ran away from volunteer work to basically frolic with a bunch of strangers. *Who am I anymore?*

"Sunshine?" He draws me back from my panic. "Your first Mardi Gras?"

"Can't you tell?"

"Yeah, but I was trying to be nice." Then there's that smile again. "I'd tell you that you get used to it, but that'd be a lie. There's no getting used to Mardi Gras, you just embrace it, you know? Let it take over—then it's smooth sailing."

I try to push away my thoughts of home and Adam and focus on Electric Blue Boy, "How do you let it take over?"

"You know . . . you just feel." He spreads his arms out wide as if that explains everything.

I laugh. "Right. Feel it."

The sun peeks out before the sky dulls again; a cloud rolls through, bringing with it another quick and delicious breeze. Soon twilight will set in, making every bit of glitter and sequins reflect brighter, like fireflies in the night. Not even the threat of storm clouds will dull them. The air has cooled down and though the music is just as loud as before, there is a calmness to it that settles in with the dimming of the sun.

"All right, all right. I'm not explaining it well enough, but it's hard to. It's like . . . you know when people tell you 'describe yourself in three words' or 'how would other people describe you' and shit?" His gestures are all over the place as he talks. "It's like that. You can't encompass a person in three words. And New Orleans—she's alive, she's a person. Hard to settle on how to describe her, but once you're in it, once you're here, you get it."

He waits for me to answer, but I'm adrift in his words, how true they feel, and his brown eyes, with flecks of gold that play off his dark skin and the kinetic lights of the carnival. His smile reaches all the way to his eyes, and they crinkle at the sides; I watch the carnival pass behind me, reflected in his irises.

Suddenly he hops off the wall. "Drink?"

"Um, yes, please."

But truthfully, no, I'd rather go back to listening to him speak about New Orleans or music or anything. Really, anything.

"I'll be right back; don't run away, okay? You looked like you might bolt when I started talking about Orleans being a person."

Nope, just staring into your gorgeous eyes and probably looking like a dolt. "I won't, I promise."

"Cool." He slips into the nearest bar, and I almost shout after him that I am sixteen and probably shouldn't be drinking anything alcoholic, but he's gone before I can and part of me kinda hopes he does bring back a beer or a *drink* drink.

I think of Adam and the swigs of Dad's whiskey and how it made him loose. How it sometimes made the shadows that followed him disappear and sometimes made them bold like the midday sun.

"You okay there, girl?" Taj settles up next to me, occupying Electric Blue's space. I realize that I know all his friend's names but not his. "You looked lost in thought there for a second, and not a very good one."

I nod. "Yeah, more like complicated and hard to get into."

Taj lays his buzok against his feet and holds his hands up with a smile.

Taj is the shortest of the guys, but there's something about him that tells me he's the life of the party. "Say no more, I won't pry."

Danny bounds over to my other side, but Domínguez seems preoccupied with a particularly flirty fairy. "I'm already soaked in sweat"—Danny points to his shirt, patches of moisture visible below his armpits—"and it ain't even eight yet."

"I told you to bring yourself a backup," Taj replies.

I'm still in a bit of a daze from Electric Blue's comment

earlier. "Are you sure that wasn't the official parade?"

Danny shakes his head. "Nah, pre-party. People are going to get their dance on until it starts around eight. Unless the sky starts falling by then."

"You mean the rain? Will they cancel if it starts raining?"

Taj shakes his head, a laugh tumbling out. "Then they'll start at eight fifteen!"

"But for real, Taj, you think that storm's going to hit us?" Danny tips his hat to a couple of girls as they walk by; they smile but keep on walking.

Taj looks up at the sky, and my gaze follows. The sky is darkening a hair's breadth at a time, but the moon is already out despite the daylight. Off in the distance there are long stretches of dark clouds ready to roll in; above us a few pitiful gray puffs threaten the evening.

"Nah, my dad says it's turning away from us and will probably die off before it gets any closer."

"Plenty close," Danny says. "From what I hear we going to feel it later in the night or early morning."

"You think people would be out here partying it up if there was a tropical storm just round the corner?"

"Hell yeah!" Danny laughs, and soon Taj is laughing as well. The wind joins in, tussling my hair.

"Wait, I thought it was just, like, rain. There's a tropical storm coming?" I interject, realizing I probably should've paid more attention to Tavis after all. But I've found it hard to think of anything outside my own drama for several weeks now.

Taj nods. "That's what one weatherman said, but everyone here knows tropical storms and hurricanes don't show up during Mid-Summer. It would be mad rude if it crashed."

"Mad rude?" Danny cackles.

"Mad rude," Taj continues, "and no storm wants to be mad rude, my friend."

Danny nods and picks up his fiddle, playing a lazy tune as he watches the revelers go by. Soon Taj joins him. "Waste of a carnival if it did. Damn waste."

"You're kidding, right? People wouldn't just—"

"Keep going?" Danny nods. "Of course they would. Nothing ruins a parade, even if we have to swim home."

As if on cue the pitiful gray cloud settles above us, releasing a cooling mist on the party below. We are the only ones who give it any mind.

Taj does a quick doggy paddle in the air. "I can't swim, man."

"I will carry you on my back." Danny turns, patting his back. "Let's go."

Taj bends his knees and takes a running leap, only to stop right before actually landing on Danny. Danny shakes his head in disappointment. I hold back a laugh, unsure if this show is for me or just a part of who they are.

"How long have you known each other?" I ask, trying

to fill the lull in conversation. The mist feels amazing, each drop cooling me down.

"All our lives; grew up together. Domínguez, your boy, and I have known each other since grade school," Danny says. "Taj's family moved here like, what?"

"Two years ago," Taj finishes, "but it feels like I was born here, you know?"

I nod even though I have no idea what he means. I've lived in my tiny little town all my life and have no idea how it would feel to live anywhere else and call it home. Not that my town feels like much of a home now.

"It's N'awlins, man," Danny continues. "She gets into your bones and you swear you were born here."

Soon Domínguez strolls right up, the accordion making the most ridiculous sounds because he's forgotten to lock it.

"I'm heading out," he says.

"Heading out where?" Taj asks.

"I've met the love of my life"—he gestures back to the fairy—"and I'm not spending another second with you *pendejos*." He looks at me. "No offense. I'm talking about them."

"None taken."

Domínguez is tall and muscular, unlike his friends who are of the reed-like variety. I would've never pegged him as someone who played the accordion at all, maybe football or something but not the accordion.

"Man, you just met the girl."

"Exactly, and I want to get to know her before we never see each other again. You know how Mardi Gras is."

Taj and Danny nod.

"Uh, what do you mean that's how Mardi Gras is?" I ask.

"It's like, something about Mardi Gras. You can be whoever you want to be and it's cool."

"Like," Danny elucidates, voice carrying over the rhythm of the day, "if you got a weird glass eye, it don't matter, on Mardi Gras you got twenty/twenty vision. If you broke—"

"You're still broke on Mardi Gras!" Taj laughs and punches Danny on the shoulder.

"True, but you don't feel it as much because the city is wide open for you."

Domínguez finishes, "For one night anything is possible. Tonight, Tinker Bell and I can be whoever we want to be; tomorrow, I might never see her again if she doesn't want to."

"That's kinda sad."

"Maybe. Sometimes you need one night to run away from shit, you know?"

"Yeah." I smile at Domínguez, because there it is, the answer I needed.

Weird how two semi-complete strangers can totally validate your actions.

As the mist travels on to bless the rest of the parade,

Domínguez nods good-bye and runs to his Tinker Bell, looping his arm around her waist, the accordion making another set of ridiculous sounds. They look happy as they disappear into the crowd.

We pause for a moment and I close my eyes, concentrating on the sound of the different bands swimming all around me. It feels like the sounds shouldn't mix—different beats, one fast, one slow, different instruments, each louder than the other, meeting each other in street corners and alleyways, talking to each other like old friends. It shouldn't work, it shouldn't—but it does, it totally does.

"Drinks!" Electric Blue comes back, offering me a half cup of beer. "I have a friend who works at the bar, and I sneaked this out for free, but I can get you some water if you want it."

"No, this is great, thank you."

"*Salud*!" he says, and we touch cups.

He pushes Danny out of the way as he sidles up beside me. Danny feigns annoyance before he goes back to people watching.

"They didn't bother you, did they?" he asks me.

"Excuse me?" Danny shouts. "How do you know she didn't bother us?"

Blue smiles, looking back at me. "I doubt that."

Yep. Permanent blush.

"I have a weird question," I say because his eyes, the feel of his skin against mine as he sits next to me is intoxicating.

The tiny little hairs on my body leap up, itching to be closer, and I need to think of something else.

"Perfect day for it."

"Okay, well, maybe not weird, but I kinda wondered how, like—how did Domínguez—"

"End up with the accordion?" he finishes for me.

"Yeah, it feels like he should be catching a football somewhere."

"Probably, if his feet were as coordinated as his hands, but they ain't." He drinks the last of his beer and turns to give me his full attention. "Now, it would be safe to say that, like most teens, you had a period of . . . growth. Whether it was awkward or not, that's up to the individual."

"Very awkward."

"Me too. Same with Danny and probably Taj, had we known him back then."

"Hey, man! I was never awkward."

"You play a buzok, my friend, and that's all I'm going to say about that." He turns back to me. "Like I was saying, we found solace in our friendship and our playing of ridiculous instruments. Because we were, and still are, pretty damn broke. And not like broke in a romantic way, just *broke* broke—so we played the instruments that we could get. Danny got the fiddle from his uncle, I got my guitar from a pawnshop as a birthday present, and Domínguez found the accordion in his mom's attic. So we made the best of what we got and here we are."

"Right, but what about the—" I point to my own arms that are devoid of any strength.

"The muscles? Growth spurt and a refusal to continue to get beat up over his love of the accordion. You aren't going to pick on a kid twice your size even if you think the accordion is funny, right?"

"Right."

He settles back on the wall, watching the crowds as they go by.

"So where are you from?"

Here it is. Where am I from? Why are you here? Where are your parents? How old are you anyway? Oh God—I close my eyes and pretend not to have heard the question, but I know he's waiting for me to answer. I stare out at the sea of masked revelers and put myself in their place, protected from the world by a cheap plastic disguise. If they can do it, I can too. I brush my shoulder against his again, and the little hairs along my arms stand on end again. I savor the feeling and take a deep breath.

"Around."

He laughs. "Around, all right. I like Around, hear it's a nice town full of scoundrels and hippies. What's your name?"

I laugh and make it a game. "What's in a name?"

"Not much, people tend to use them to refer to one

another . . . or maybe that was a trick question and your name is really Rose . . . is your name Rose? Do you smell as sweet?"

His face inches closer.

"No, though that is a good guess."

"I try."

A group of papier-mâché oysters stop in front of us, offering a strand of pearlescent green beads. Before I can reply yes or no, one of them drapes it around my neck and runs away.

"Thank you!" I shout after them, marveling at their paper-shaping talents.

"Suits you," Electric Blue says, fiddling with the beads—*be cool*—before he takes another swig from the already empty cup. "Okay, okay. So, no name. No place to call home. You're a real girl, right, not a figment of my imagination?"

I choke on my beer at the implication that he would ever imagine me.

"I have a name and"—I pause—"a home; I just don't want to think of either tonight, if that makes sense."

"Complicated?"

I swirl the beer in my cup, barely half gone. "So complicated thinking of it just a little causes it all to come crashing down, you know? I thought maybe . . . maybe New Orleans could drown it out, at least the parts I don't like."

I take a last sip, sticking out my tongue. Never really liked the taste of beer—I'm usually ready to throw it out after one mouthful.

He looks at me then, a slow nod. "Yeah, I know what you mean."

"You do?"

"Yeah—feels like, every time you think about it you're just like that, straight in the deep end, drowning." He reaches over for my cup and tosses both in a nearby trash can that's minutes away from overflowing. "How about a deal?"

"Deal?"

He jumps up to face me, excitement in his eyes. "Just for tonight. No real names, no baggage—unless we want to—no 'I'll text you later' or promises to call. Just two people—"

"Two people?" Taj interjects. "What are we, chopped liver?"

"Fine, just SOME PEOPLE in the general vicinity enjoying New Orleans and their company together for one night and nothing else. You can leave at any time—and vice versa, should you turn out to be a crazy sociopath, have unsavory intentions toward my person, or should you just be very, very boring. How about that?"

He holds out his hand, offering up a night of peace and freedom. I shake on it.

"But for serious, what should I call you, Sunshine? I

can't be yelling out 'hey you' or 'hey girl' or 'hey fairy girl' in this crowd—it might be funny for the first minute until I get slapped in the face or something."

"Why would you get slapped in the face?"

"It would be a misunderstanding, obviously."

"Obviously." I tuck a hair behind my ear. "You could call me Sunshine if you want." I like the way it sounds coming out of his mouth. "I like that."

He considers this. "Maybe." Suddenly his eyes still on mine. "But only sometimes. Sometimes Sunshine and sometimes . . . Lila."

"Why Lila?"

"Um." He clears his throat. "Means 'night' in Arabic. Figured sometimes sunshine, sometimes night." He shrugs his shoulders, his eyes finding mine, lingering. "Too silly?"

"No." My breath catches. "Not too silly."

He beams. "Fantastic! My name is—"

"Miles," I finish for him.

"Miles?" He feels the name out on his tongue. "Like Miles Davis?"

"Um, yeah, and Miles Kane. Both of them actually. The way you play reminds me of them. I mean, I've only seen you play once, but it made me think of this recording my dad has of Miles Davis, but, like, I have a really good friend who's into British music, and she used to show these videos of Miles Kane and . . ." Now I'm babbling. "Um . . . yeah, like Miles Davis. Cool?"

He's trying not to laugh. I can tell.

"Cool."

I smile and forget that my hand is still warm in his, up until Taj and Danny interject once more.

"How come we don't get fancy code names?"

Miles lets go, and for a moment my hand feels cold and alone. I shrug away the thought and put it back in my pocket.

"You've already been introduced."

"I think we should get fancy code names, and backstories, don't you, Taj?"

Taj puffs out his chest. "Absolutely; I'd like to be Denis."

"Denis?" Danny says. "What? No, man. Pick something decent like Clark Kent or Conan."

"Fine, I'll be Kent."

"Nah, man. Clark Kent. You can't just be Kent—shit's too white."

"Man, you white," Taj shouts.

"Exactly, I should know."

They continue on like this for a bit, and I swear my heart grows lighter by the minute. I look up to see Miles staring at me, a soft smile on his lips, like he'd planned this all along. He reaches his hand out to me, and for a moment I see all the possibilities waiting. I take it.

"Let's go, Midsummer Boys. The night awaits."

Shakespeare on the Roof

"MAN, WHERE ARE WE GOING?" DANNY YELLS OVER THE WAVES of sound that flow around us.

"Gotta find a prime spot before the parade starts." I feel the tug of Miles's hand pulling me along; to my left Danny keeps the crowd from tearing us apart and setting me adrift at sea. Taj takes the rear. If the night is truly awaiting, we are going to be so late.

I push against the people around me, still in a bit of shock. How does New Orleans have this much energy? Above us the electricity flows in a web of cables that cut across the sky and swing back and forth with the wind. Should I get lost, I wonder if the pattern above me will be just as useful as the stars were to those sailing across the seas?

After what feels like an eternity of weaves and sharp turns and wings getting snagged, Miles stops and I collide into his back. "Sorry!" I push myself away and try not to think of how close we were and how good it felt. His body is firm and warm, and I wonder if I could stage another collision just to bump into him again. I force the edges of my mouth not to form a smile and look down at the ground. It's still there, good.

"Why did we stop? What's the plan?" Oh God I sound lame. *Just go with the flow, Jules.* "Not that there needs to be one for everything, you know?"

The corner of Miles's mouth quirks. "Relax, I have a strategy."

Taj rolls his eyes.

"What's your plan then?" Miles retorts.

"It's Mid-Summer!" Taj motions around him as if we'd somehow walked through all these people and missed that fact. "Go where the mood takes you. Not everything has to have an itinerary, maestro."

Miles claps Taj on the shoulder. "All right, does your going where the mood takes you include getting some sustenance?"

As if on cue my stomach grumbles, thankfully drowned out by the sounds around us.

"It does now," Taj replies.

· · ·

SEVERAL BUMPS AND close calls where wings snagged on strangers' costumes and we're leaning over the rooftop of one of the buildings along Oak, looking down at the street below, then out to the burning sunset. There have been several fires in New Orleans history—what we stand on now is built over the ashes of one of its previous incarnations. I wonder if at some point the people who lived here could not bear to watch the sun set, as it lit the sky on fire.

Miles nudges my shoulder, motioning to where the night has taken us. "Not bad, eh?"

Not bad? "It's amazing." I can see everyone and every-thing. Two more baby floats pass by as I watch. One's a crazy-looking octopus painted in fluorescent colors—I have a feeling it's made to really shine later in the night—and I can't figure out the second float, but it looks like someone took a lot of paper flowers, threw glitter on them, and set them on wheels.

A man with a glitter tartan looks up from the flower float. Finding my eyes, he smiles and winks. Charming.

"How did you get them to let us up here?"

Taj plops down behind me. "You know how it is. Some smooth talking. Promises you don't intend to keep."

Danny weaves around Taj, rustling his hair before jumping away from his swinging hand. "Or a friend of my mom's owns the building."

"Ah."

"Come on." Danny motions to the bundles of lumpy paper bags we'd scavenged before coming up, and we pile around them. "Let's eat before it starts."

There's a particularly oil-soaked bag right in the middle of the others that I don't recognize. Must have come from Danny, who'd disappeared for twenty minutes before we reunited. Taj leans down and tears it open. "Café Beignet or Du Monde?" he asks Danny.

"Beignets?" I've been dying to try beignets—fried dough is one of my favorite things in the world—but hadn't had the chance. Another one of Tavis's promises not delivered and number one on my list of things to do in New Orleans. "We are going to have beignets?" I perk up, ready to tear into whichever bag holds those delicious little treats. I hadn't noticed any of the boys stopping to buy them, and I have no idea how they managed to sneak it by me.

"Hell yeah." Danny wags his eyebrows then turns to Taj. "Neither. Too far. These are from the local joint a couple of blocks away."

We begin to break into the bags, arranging the food in front of us. Along with the beignet there are some deli-meat-type sandwiches called mufa-something or other.

"But just to be clear, if I had, I would've gotten Café Beignet," Danny says.

Taj checks his head in mock disgust. "Why are we even friends, man?"

"Aww." Danny takes Taj down with a giant hug.

"Hey, man, be cool!" Taj shouts from the ground. "Be. Cool."

There's an ache in my stomach. Watching Danny and Taj joke around makes me miss Kara and Em so much. For a moment I try to forget how much I've screwed up my friendships as Taj pushes Danny off him, straightening his shirt and pretending to be mad as hell. I watch Miles smile at his friends, chuckling; when he catches me watching the grin gets even bigger. He gestures toward his friends as if to say, "What can you do?"

"How many shifts did you have to promise for all of this?" Miles asks as he takes the Bottom hat off and tosses it down next to him.

"Just one," Danny replies, then pauses, "on Saturday."

"Ouch." Miles pats Danny on the shoulder. "A great sacrifice."

Indeed, but looking around at the awesome spread I kinda think it is worth it. "Thanks, Danny. These look amazing."

"It's so beautiful it's making me cry," Taj jokes, holding back fake tears as he basks in the glory of our feast.

"Thank you so much, really; you didn't have to bring me along and feed me."

"You're welcome!" Taj says as Miles hits his shoulder.

"Don't worry about it. My mama always said you can learn a lot from a person by breaking bread together," Miles says.

"You can? How?"

"Actually I have no idea. But she's really big on the idea, and my mama is never wrong. So, who's going to dive in first?"

No one makes the first move, and I don't know why. This has to be the most delicious array of delicacies I've seen in a long time. I break the trance and dive for a beignet before the sugar becomes an oil-soaked glob. I open my mouth to take a bite of the delicious goodness, and a puff of powder shoots up into my lungs, making me cough for a solid minute.

Danny pats me on the back, offering me water. "Rookie mistake. Don't breathe in before taking a bite, you'll have sugar in your lungs for days."

After my embarrassing first try I finally get it right, and when I bite through the mountain of sugar into the crisp skin of the beignet I am automatically in love.

"I could eat these until I die."

"Not a bad way to go," Miles says as he watches me lick the remainder of the sugar from my fingers. I'm not sure if he's talking about the beignets or me. The blush in my cheeks says the latter.

IT'S LESS THAN an hour till the parade starts. I am stuffed as I help the boys gather all our garbage, shoving it into a plastic bag before anything gets carried off by the wind.

I can still taste the delicious sugar on my lips when Miles asks, "Salty or sweet?"

"Hmm?"

He motions to where moments before our feast was laid out for us. "Salty or sweet?"

"Sweet." My tongue darts out, licking the side of my mouth, a bit of sugar still stuck to my lips.

Miles's gaze lingers. "Yeah, me too." He looks away, a playful smirk on his face. "I can down at least a dozen beignets if no one stops me. What's your favorite sweet?"

"Oh, I'm really bad at favorites." I trace the silhouette of his face as the lights from below play across his skin. I turn away before he catches me staring.

"That's what people say at first. Then before you know it they're going on and on about pecan pie." Sticking his hands in his pockets—looking ever the rogue—Miles leans over the edge and grins at me. "Or should I say *peeee-can* pie."

I shake my head. "I'm not kidding, I have a hard time picking just a few of my favorite things."

He chuckles, singing, "'Bright copper kettles and warm woolen mittens,'" before shrugging. "My mom loves musicals." He taps a finger against his temples. "Pretty much have them all memorized." At the edge of the building the world below bustles with life. "We've got time to kill, Lila. We can sit around and enjoy the silence, or we can get to know each other." He whistles, calling over Danny and Taj.

They trudge over. "Hey, man. I told you we don't answer to whistles," Taj says.

"You literally just did," Miles points out.

"To tell you it's the last time."

"Whatever." Miles waves away the argument. "Favorite dessert. Go."

Taj licks his lips. "Fried bananas with a scoop of ice cream. My dad learned to make it when we lived in DC. There was this little Thai shop a couple blocks away."

"Peach cobbler," Danny chimes in. "The way my gran used to make it, with tons of sugar."

"See?" Miles turns back, waiting for me to join in, amusement in his eyes. "Not that hard. Let's try it again. Favorite dessert?"

Taj hops up and down. "Oh yesss, we playing Questions, Questions?"

"Questions, Questions?"

"Just like it sounds," Taj says. "Helps pass time."

"So does a book."

Miles perks, leaning in closer. "You got one in that bag?"

"No." I playfully shove him away with a finger. "But I know some by heart."

"Do you now, which ones?"

Oh God, which one is least embarrassing? I run through the list—none, awesome. A sigh. "Harry Potter."

"Yo, I took that damn Pottermore test and it told me I was a Hufflepuff. What kind of bullshit is that?" Taj shouts.

"You don't want to be a Huffle?" I ask.

He puffs up his chest. "Slytherin all the way, baby."

Behind him Danny shakes his head and mouths the word "Hufflepuff." I snort, covering my mouth.

"What, you don't think I have Slytherin tendencies?" Taj asks.

Miles tugs at my shirt, touching skin to skin. It sends a shock down my body. "What else?"

I rub my shoulder, tapping down the thousands of tiny hairs standing on end. "Well, I don't actually like the play, but I played Juliet in our school production of *Romeo and Juliet*."

Perking up, a sly smirk spreads across his lips. "Oh really?"

MOMENTS LATER I'M dead—well, fake dead, roofied by a priest who "meant well" (Did I mention I'm not a huge fan of this play? Made for a lot of arguments between me and the so-called director)—regretting the angle of my body on Danny's lap. *This will hurt later.* Performing an abridged version of *Romeo and Juliet* on a rooftop was not where I thought this night was going, but new Julie doesn't back away from a dare. Danny was tumbling through his best Romeo-in-the-crypt speech, bawling, holding my dead body, which shakes with such a force every time he cries that it is nearly impossible not to dissolve into church giggles, but I manage.

"'Here's to my love,'" Danny bellows, fake agony ringing from his voice. He is the worst actor, and it's fantastic. "Oh true, uh, crap."

"Apothecary," I stage-whisper from my fake coma.

"Right," he breaks, his muffled laugh tickling my belly. "'Oh true apothecary. Thy drugs are quick. Thus with a kiss I die.'"

I did not think this through. My eyes open just a bit, trying to sneak a peek at Miles. My heart flutters. If I was going to kiss someone I just met, I'd rather it be . . .

I feel Danny lean down, pressing a quick peck on my cheek before he lets out a death gargle and keens forward on top of me. I wait a moment, composing myself before my eyes open.

To my left, Taj gasps. "She's alive. Damn." Which almost sends me back into a fit of giggles. Miles swats him in the belly, and he quiets down.

"'O comfortable friar!'" I continue. "'Where is my lord?'"

"He's, like, right there," Taj whispers to Miles, earning him another swat. He quiets down, but it's too late. Danny has the church giggles, and now I'm infected as well.

He rolls off me just as Taj and Miles jump to their feet, clapping. Danny helps me up, and we take a bow.

"Not bad, Juliet." It's so close to my actual name that my breath catches for a moment when Miles says it. I try and shift the focus, watching the way his hips move and angle toward me; I let my cheeks flush watching how his finger hooks in his belt loop.

"That's exactly what my drama teacher said," I reply, hopefully not sounding horribly bitter. "I was the understudy, but I think, like, the pity understudy."

"I don't believe it." His hand leaves his hip, touching my arm for a moment, before he pulls back, sticking his hand in his hair. It's a move I recognize; the want, need, to keep touching, skin to skin, but knowing that it's probably not a good idea. "When you said, 'O, swear not by the moon, th' inconstant moon, that monthly changes in her circle orb. Lest that thy love prove likewise variable,' it took my breath away." The words flow like he's said them all his life.

"Whoa" escapes before I can stop myself. "I mean, you trying to get the job?"

"Only if you'll be my Romeo," he says. A quick smile reaches up to his eyes, an invitation. Damn, the guy is pure charm. I wish I had a cup or a scarf or a friggin' sweater to hide my blushing face in because I am not smooth enough for this boy.

"I think Danny would make a better Romeo," I say.

Without missing a beat Miles turns to Danny and

shouts, "'O Romeo, Romeo! Wherefore art thou, Romeo?'"

"What?" Danny replies before going back to the convo he was having with Taj.

"See?" Miles continues. "Amateur." He ventures closer. "What do you say, Sunshine, encore performance? My iambic is a bit rusty, but I think I can manage."

Yes. Absolutely. But no words actually leave my lips. A cacophony of sound blasts from the streets below us. Danny rushes over, snagging Miles's forearm and pulling him away. "It's started. There's a better view over here."

Miles reaches for me, our hands link, excitement flowing from one to the other. We all lean over the edge of the building. The writhing mass of people below us gather like atoms preparing to split.

And at the front of the assembly stands the Krewe of OAK, who put on Mid-Summer, dressed as blazing suns of all sizes. Golden, red, and yellow rays reaching out so far they could chase the storm clouds away. The trumpets build, gathering up the drums, waking the cymbals; the suns ruffle their rays like mating birds. I lean my chin down on the ledge, narrowing my eyes until they become stars shooting across a night sky and planets colliding into each other on their way to making life. The boys are talking, commenting on costumes; I drift in and out of the conversation whenever Miles bumps against me. His presence keeps me awake; I feel so alive next to him.

The revelers continue on, some look up, wave, and

beckon us down, while others toss strands of beads up to us. My legs itch to join in. I shift, restless now. What was once a dense and far too crowded thoroughfare has thinned out enough to slip into the madness. I straighten, decision made, and stand.

All eyes shift to me, waiting. "I wanna go down."

Taj and Danny look at each other, waiting on Miles, who in turn is observing me. I'm practically on the tip of my toes, bouncing, filled with energy. I can see myself among the stars, colliding, dancing, falling.

He nods, and we flow down the steps into the Milky Way.

A Face in the Crowd

MILES AND I REMAIN IN EACH OTHER'S SIGHTS, BUT WE SWING and dance and revel with those around us. We are among the gods, and we are below the seas with the brightest fish, fins swaying to the beat. I hear the strums of a banjo and follow. Miles plays for everyone, I realize, but every time our eyes lock, I think he's playing just for me.

Somewhere along our celebration it starts to rain. The clouds, once off in the distance, catch up, attempting to spoil our fun. But no such luck. We welcome the rain, a cool blessing against our overheated skin despite the night air; we throw our hands up, streaks of glitter traveling down our bodies, and continue on. After a few minutes the rain stops and the crowd cheers as we parade on.

We are far from where we started, somewhere near the Maple Leaf Bar in what Taj says is a neighborhood called Carrollton, although we can't get within ten feet of the entrance. A dense halo of people surrounds the door, and so far we've had no luck getting inside. Our little troupe makes its way to a relatively quiet street corner, watching the rest of the costumes go by as my sore legs, blood pumping, settle down.

"Danny?" someone calls from behind us, and Danny's smile falls, his shoulders slump. "Uh, back in a second, guys."

Danny is up and off before I can even see who called. He runs over to a tall guy with a shaved head, neatly trimmed (and sparse) beard, and a shirt that shows off his fit arms. As Danny nears, the guy reaches out a hand to rest against his shoulder—a gesture that I now associate too much with sympathy—but Danny slips away, remaining close yet out of reach.

"What's . . . ," I start to say.

"Ex," Taj answers before I manage to finish. "Didn't end well."

"Oh." I watch the two of them together, mesmerized by the back and forth and this new discovery about Danny. "But he was totally flirting with a girl earlier, wasn't he?"

"Probably." Miles shrugs. "And with you too. Danny likes to flirt with anyone who will flirt back really. Doesn't mean anything."

65

I nod, already 100 percent invested in the dance between Danny and his former boyfriend, one moving forward, expectant, the other stepping back, refusing. If his ex had hoped for a quick and casual conversation, then this wasn't it. The ex inches in closer, trying to get Danny to talk to him, but Danny will barely look him in the eye. Small touches are avoided and rebuffed.

"How old is he?"

"Nineteen going on asshole"—Taj scowls—"from the way he treated Danny."

"I'm fine," I hear Danny say over the music before he shrugs off another attempt at a connection. I whip my head back to Taj and Miles, who must have been eavesdropping as well. Not that they have anything to be sorry about—they actually know Danny and what's been going on, and I'm just someone they met today who has no right to interlope on this conversation.

The ex storms off, and Danny is left standing alone among inebriated partygoers who stumble around him as if he were a part of the street itself. I feel the urge to stand, but Miles is up by Danny's side before I feel him move. He puts a hand on Danny's shoulder and leans close, saying something I can't hear. Danny nods, and they walk back in our direction.

This is more than I should be allowed to see, isn't it? I'm a stranger, an outsider, and yet I feel a part of the group. Perhaps this is the Mid-Summer effect, a connection that pops into your life if only for the moment, igniting memories that continue to resonate.

When Danny returns to our side I try and forget what I've just witnessed, but I can't help but ask, "Everything okay?"

Danny smiles—the kind of smile that says, "Let's fool the demons." "No," he answers, "but I'm told it gets better."

"What does?"

"Heartbreak." He offers us another sad smile that makes me hope it does, before he shakes himself like a dog. "Shaking it off. No time for this drama. What's next for the night? Maple Leaf has a cover charge and a protective layer of bodies, so that's out."

"We could head over to another party," Taj says. "There's plenty of them around."

Another party feels like more of the same. My body itches for something new, different. There must be more to New Orleans than dancing.

"How"—I clear my throat—"about we walk around a bit? I haven't seen much of New Orleans."

"You want a tour, Lila?" Miles turns back to Taj and Danny. "What do you say, boys? Tour?"

Danny and Taj shrug at the same time. They are totally in sync, which is quite amusing.

Miles claps his hands. "That's the enthusiasm I'm looking for."

"Madame La Laurie?" Danny suggests.

"No!" Taj shouts.

"Why not?"

"Man, f—" Taj cut off his curse halfway. "Forget Madame La Laurie! That shit freaks me out."

Miles laughs and leans in. "Taj will be freaked out for most of this trip, I'll tell you that right now."

"Let's not pretend y'all weren't raised to respect the spirits and histories of New Orleans more than I was. I've been here two years, and even I know not to mess with this city."

"Is that true?" I look at Miles, and when I can't hold his gaze for long I turn to Danny. "Do you all believe in ghosts?"

"It's hard not to believe in something in New Orleans. Ghosts, spirits, vampires." He wiggles his fingers, imitating I don't know, a ghost? He drops his hands and shrugs. "It's kind of like breathing here. And even if you don't believe, you don't go around traipsing in cemeteries and kicking over gravestones. There's a level of . . ."

"Respect," Danny offers.

"Fear," Taj adds.

"Tradition," Danny again, making it into a test.

"All of the above," Miles says. "It's just . . . you know?"

"Not really." I shake my head.

I can feel Miles's breath on my neck. "Don't worry, Sunshine, by the end of tonight you will."

His reaches over, fingers wrapping around my wrists, his touch speaking of the night ahead—a night to live and forget.

God, just let me forget. A silent prayer I recite to myself. Already the thoughts of Adam and my life back home threaten to sneak in like water through a crevice. I know that if I turn my phone on I'll have triple the texts I had before. My head starts to pound when I think of all the unanswered messages piling up, pouring out of my phone, and wrapping themselves around me. They repeat like a broken record, Where are you?, until I push them back down.

"Promise?"

Miles holds out his hand, flipping it over to loop his pinkie with mine. "Promise." He holds me there, his eyes on mine—I think—until I believe him. Idly I notice that I'm tracing the line of the bracelet he wears on his wrist. Fine and delicate, it's refreshingly cooler than my skin feels right now.

"Yo, is that Amy and the girls?" Taj points with his chin off into the crowd.

Miles's hand drops, and his head snaps back to Taj, then scans the crowd, his eyes narrowing. "Yeah." His brow furrows for a moment before he wipes the worry from his face—it's a conscious change, a kind of mask because I can still read the tension in his body. Something I've become rather adept at the last couple of months. Hunched shoulders, bowed heads . . . just because you are not speaking does not mean you are silent.

I don't tell Miles this, that I can read him and know the bright smile he flashes back to me isn't quite as honest as he'd like it to be. A flush of disappointment creeps in, tugging my shoulders down as I curl inward. Somewhere behind me a tuba blares, kicking me out of my spiral and blasting away the feeling of disenchantment. I don't care how much truth there is to this night. I'm not looking for truth, I'm looking to escape, so I take his smile and move past it.

"Who's Amy?"

"Friend of a friend."

Danny and Taj exchange glances. I'm smart enough to realize that either Amy is his girlfriend or friends with his girlfriend or someone he hooked up with. If I was being optimistic I'd guess his sister, maybe? Either way Amy is not someone Miles wants me to meet.

"Is she coming on the ghost tour?" I keep my tone light and innocent.

Miles shrugs, moving us under a balcony where it is considerably darker. I follow his gaze to a group of girls dressed up like birds. It's unclear if they were part of the parade or are just heading out to join the parties—their effervescent energy seems natural as they make their way through the square. Miles shifts farther back into the shadows, while Taj and Danny stand in front of us.

"Who are you hiding from?" I whisper in Miles's ear.

"What?" He turns to me, his face so close to mine. His eyes dart to my lips, realizing how close they are to his.

I roll my eyes. "You're hiding from someone, I can tell."

"Not at all."

"You are far from subtle."

Miles is about to deny it when there are shouts from the girls. They've spotted Taj and Danny, who have made no effort to hide. Miles's shoulders visibly slump, and I want to laugh at his misery when my own face falls because out there, in the crowd behind the girls, is Tavis.

"Fuck."

Run

My heart is somewhere in my stomach, and I slide back as far into the shadows as I can. When my heart returns to its proper position, it's beating quite fast.

Calm down, I tell myself. Maybe it's not Tavis, maybe I'm seeing things, and it's just my guilt getting the better of me. I shouldn't have run from the site like that. My parents must be worried sick about me, and they have so much to worry about already with Adam and . . . and everything. I can feel Tavis's clammy hands on me, pulling me into a hug, telling me how disappointed he is. Taking me home to the closed doors and unplugged television, to the grating friction of fork against knife as no words are spoken across the dinner table. My hands clench.

I check again, maybe I'm imagining things. It can't be him. There are at least five out of the seven deadly sins happening around us right now, and I can't imagine Tavis willfully throwing himself in the vicinity of it. My gaze finds him again—it's definitely him. Oh God—and in that moment his eyes lock with mine. His lips form my name, "Julie," as he pushes through the crowds. His way is slow, the sea of revelers doesn't part for him, and as he moves he is shoved back, the people returning push for push.

I breathe in and out, tracking the beating of my heart, realizing that I am no longer scared. My heart is not pumping with fear but anger. How dare Tavis be here? How dare he try to take me away? I need this. I need this and I just got it and now I have to give it up? No.

No.

A man twice Tavis's size is shoving a finger in his chest. Tavis has his hands up, trying to calm him down. This is it. This is the moment. A wicked smile spreads across my face and I turn to Miles, snatching his hand into mine.

"I'm not ready for this to end," I say, hoping Miles understands. I glance at Tavis one more time. Miles follows my look; Tavis is waving at me frantically. Our eyes dart to the girls, happily chatting as they make their way over to Taj and Danny. Our night is moments from collapsing in front of us.

Miles squeezes my hand. "Me neither."

73

"Get ready to run," I say.

Taj and Danny turn back to us, their brows scrunched in question.

"Intercept!" I yell to the boys and dash away with Miles, pulling him behind me through the crowd and around the corner. We run, feet stomping down the cobblestones, pushing past fish, birds, stars, and yelling back apologies as we escape. In alleys we run past revelers in compromising positions, they yell at us for interrupting their fun, a laugh tumbles out. Street after street we escape, hands clasped together, speeding our way toward a night of promise. If my legs ache I don't notice, they continue pumping as the houses around me shift, their intricacies multiplying as we go along. Miles loses his hat at some point. It flies off his head and into the crowd, claimed by another reveler. At corners we hop on tiptoes waiting for lights to change before dashing across. When we are far enough from our troubles, we cut between two buildings and collapse against each other.

I drop Miles's hand, placing mine on my knees, calming my lungs.

There is no sign of Taj, Danny, the girls, or Tavis.

I smile.

Between breaths Miles's chest convulses, a soft chuckle then a full-blown laugh.

It's fantastic and full of energy. It travels across the

alley and pulls my own from my lips. I want to go on like this forever.

Calming down, Miles straightens up. "What am I hiding from? What are YOU hiding from, Sunshine?"

"Nothing."

He waits for me to say more, and when I don't he nods but doesn't drop my gaze. "Yeah, me too." He still gulps large breaths, and I watch his chest rise and fall; he starts shaking his head like something doesn't sit right. "Liar. You panicked and ran."

"*We* ran."

"True, true." He nods, staring back at whatever we left behind. "I wanted to get out of there."

"Why? Was she your girlfriend?"

Miles pushes away from the wall he is recuperating on, approaching me. He stands a whole seven inches above me—I hadn't realized how tall he is until now, or how short I was in comparison. He must be at least six feet something, while I am a very respectable five-five. When he looks down to meet my eyes I sense the invitation to close the gap.

"You first. Tell me why you ran, and I'll tell you why I ran."

He inches closer; I fight the instinct to push him away because that would require more touching, although at the moment, it's exactly what I wanted.

"No. No baggage, remember?"

He steps back. "No baggage."

There's a faint buzz from his phone, and he pulls it out. I touch mine, still in my pocket, and fight old Julie for the urge to turn it back on.

"It's Danny and Taj. They got roped into a party. Guess we're on our own, Lila."

Alone with Electric Blue and no buffer. *Breathe.*

"Their loss," I reply.

"Yeah." Miles reaches under his shirt to scratch his stomach—I follow the movement and catch a glimpse of the sparse hairs on his abdomen before he rearranges the strap on his banjo. "Their loss."

Miles extends his arm, and as I loop mine around his, my mind keeps roaming back to the flash of skin. The thought of it makes me happy. Oh God. This is why people compose sonnets, isn't it? *An Ode to Miles's Abs.*

"Where to?" he asks.

A flood of places pop into my mind. Too many to count. Old houses. Food. Cemeteries. Food. Stores. Food. *You JUST ate, belly!* I want to see it all but don't know where to start or where anything is and whether or not they are within walking distance, which I'm assuming will be our major mode of transportation.

"How far are we from the cemeteries?"

"Ah, you want to see Marie Laveau's grave, right?"

"That's the famous one?"

"It is, but cemeteries are not a good place to be at night, at least not for us."

"Really? Why?"

"Shady shit mostly. Taj got jumped there once, which knowing Taj is not that hard to believe. He has a way of getting into trouble." He runs his hand over his hair; it changes just a bit as he shapes it. "He was supposed to meet this girl, but he got stood up, then mugged, so overall not a great night for him."

"Oh." Checking it off the list then.

"Yeah, so stick to the daylight when visiting the dead. Much safer for the living."

"Safe sounds good, I guess." But I can't hide the disappointment from my voice.

"You say *safe*," Miles teases, "but I hear *boring*. What is it that you really want?"

I want to go and let the night unfold before us. No thoughts. No plans.

"I don't care," I say, tugging him closer, "and I don't think you should care either."

"How's that?"

"I think we should just walk, pick a way and go. Not overthink it or anything. If I'm going to let go tonight, you are as well, Miles."

"That might be a bit hard for me . . . my mind thrives

on plans," Miles replies.

I unloop my arm from his—regrettably—to face him. "Trust me."

I step away from him, bringing my arms to my chest. "Count to five, then stop me."

"Stop you?" Miles tilts his head to the side, intrigued.

I close my eyes, take a deep breath, and spin.

"One." I hear Miles count as the world shifts around me. "Two."

This is it, I think. "Three." I'm shaking off all the worries, emerging anew. "Four." I extend my hand out. "Five." Hands on my hips, strong, I lean back into Miles, my other hand reaching up to his neck, fingers brushing his hair, breath steadying. My eyes open and follow my hand down our path. "That way."

"You sure?" he whispers, hands coming fully around my waist turning me to face him.

I catch him calculating our route in his head, brow creasing. "Don't think," I whisper. With a finger I erase the horizontal lines across his forehead. "Please, just trust me. Whatever the night brings."

His grip tightens around my waist. A silent yes.

WE STEP BACK out onto the streets, feeling the beat of something just around the corner. Miles's phone buzzes again. I pull it out of his reach.

"No phones."

"No phones?"

"No interruptions, just you and me and New Orleans." I hope my tone is as playful as I feel.

He turns the phone over in his hands. "Okay, but I gotta tell Taj and D." He types something quickly and turns the phone off. "We'll need a meeting place. Something popular, like Jackson Square."

"Why?"

"In case we get separated."

"Planning on running again?"

He squeezes my arm, and I squeeze back before I have time to think about it. His touch is warm and welcoming despite the heat.

"Only if you run with me."

I AM THAT MERRY WANDERER
OF THE NIGHT

The world it jests
it plays for bets.
It takes a soul
or two at best.

So quell your fears,
and take flight
let's be wanderers
just for tonight.

Come, come away,
to the evening that awaits.
Come, come away,
to the evening that awaits.

Pack your troubles
though they wail and storm
tonight's for lovers
no room for scorn.

And when she drinks
against her lips
the night alight on her fingertips.

So quell your fears,
and take flight
let's be wanderers
just for tonight.

Come, come away,
to the evening that awaits.
Come, come away,
to the evening that awaits.

Never waste
a single breath,
a night to wake
no time to fret,
a night to live,
a merry wanderer ready to forgive.

The Holy Name of Jesus

LOYOLA CATHEDRAL IS OPEN, AND IT SHOULD NOT BE. THIS FACT is a very welcome development, since Miles and I have just escaped from the clutches of several very drunk frat-boy types whose idea of a costume is simply to unzip their pants. Granted, the having to escape part is my fault; sarcasm and a man's penis size don't go hand in hand . . . so to speak.

They are about a block behind us, and I make the mistake of turning my head to see where they are. The most vocal of the four catches my eye and attempts to smile, but it just looks like he's unsure of whether or not he has to vomit. This doesn't stop him from shouting in my direction.

"Offer is still open, baby-uh-cupcakes-and-cream-heart." He reaches down to grope himself. I stick my pinkie finger up in the air, wiggle it, and shake my head.

Overall not my best idea.

Hence I am more than elated that the Holy Name of Jesus Parish (official name) is open even though the last Mass was at six that evening. Perhaps it's open all the time. My church back home started locking its doors around eight after a particular set of rowdy teens decided to have a midnight rager.

I wish I knew more about architecture. Words, anything really, to describe what I'm seeing. The only word I can think of is breathtaking.

The temperature shifts as we enter and quietly close the doors behind us. My eyes travel to the large stone pillars and up to the arches and the expansive ceiling, perfect for sound to bounce back and forth. Stained glass captures the lamplight from the outside, bringing the stories to life.

The squeak of our sneakers travels up and up, fading as we walk. There are no other sounds; the silence makes me nervous after the vibrancy of the streets. My memories threaten to slip out without the Mid-Summer energy to hold them in. I concentrate on how the light radiates from the archways, glowing, breathing, and warm. If I close my eyes I can hear Father Lopez giving his Sunday sermon.

I see Adam sitting on a bench, and my step catches. When I open my eyes, he is gone. *The doors shouldn't have been open,* I think, *and we should not be here.*

"I don't think this was a good idea."

"Want to go back outside with the drunks?"

I shake my head, pushing old Julie away. Not letting her creep into every thought. This is new Julie's night. No squares permitted.

"It's a place of worship, pretty sure we're allowed."

"Only during business hours," I quip.

His laugh travels the way of my footsteps, and though it fades, the memory of it lingers and lightens my spirit.

"Sad, right? That you can't just walk into a church when you need one. Isn't that the purpose of them? Sanctuary and all." He faces the expanse and yells, "Sanctuary! Sanctuary!"

I shake my head and he gets louder, so I reach up and clasp a hand over his mouth, his words echoing. Somewhere a door bursts open behind the giant pillars and we both Red-Light freeze like carefree children.

"Green light!" I whisper, and we duck behind the nearest pew.

"Nicely done," he says, crouching, and I beam. You're not always lucky enough to find your Red Light, Green Light soul mate. We can't see anything. I wait for footsteps but nothing comes. We hear the door close, creaking, and we are plunged back into silence.

"Maybe we should go," I say again.

"Let's sit a while; it's quieter here than in all of Orleans. We'll miss it later."

It's true, I feel calmer the more I think about it. Miles takes my hand, and we walk over to a set of pews, toward the back, as hidden as possible.

"It's quiet like this that pulls out every truth in your soul," he says, then turns to me. "Can you feel it?"

I can, but I don't want to. I'm not quick enough to hide the emotions flashing across my face, and I know Miles sees my fear, my sadness, before I can hide them away.

"Okay?" he asks, and I nod.

Lies, lies, lies. But I can live with these lies for tonight, though perhaps one truth will help. "I just think my truths are good where they are right now."

"Fair enough," he says.

I take a seat, and Miles lies down on the pew behind me. Part of me wishes he'd taken the seat next to me, but something about the distance feels right at the moment. Having him so close for so long is making it hard to think.

Leaning his banjo to one side, Miles stretches out on the pew. "Yeah, this is more like it." A wink. I roll my eyes.

"So." He sits back up, a smile on his face. "Questions, Questions time!"

Miles's excitement for the night feels like a constant thing, effortless, natural. Makes me want to drown in it. "Okay."

He shifts toward me, resting his head on the back of my pew, a wicked little grin on his face. "Pets."

"Not a one." I picture a dog with the same amount of energy as Miles bounding in front of him as they walk.

"Really, you've never had any pets?"

"Not even a goldfish."

"Strict parents?"

"I guess. I'm allergic to dogs so I had to set myself up for a lifetime of disappointment. I don't think cats are supposed to be pets—more like very expensive roommates that occasionally look like they want to kill you."

"Birds?"

I shiver. "No way. Have you seen the movie *The Birds*? They can't be trusted either. Besides, allergies."

"How do you cope?"

"Kleenex and a deep sense of longing. Lots of waving at dogs from across the street. You?"

He leans back on his pew, hands behind his head. "I had a cat—or a roommate, as you say. It was a street cat that I fed once, just once, and it would come over every day after that. On occasion it would let me pet it out of the kindness of its heart. You like Shakespeare, yes?"

"Hey." I wag my finger at him. "It's my turn."

"Do your worst."

I make a show of thinking over my options. "Let's see, politics, world news . . ."

He waits patiently, watching me count the options on

my fingers like a first grader until I decide. "Favorite food."

He scratches his chin in deep thought. "Now, I know I should say something N'awlins based, I really should, but it's actually pizza. Chicago style. Can't help it." He points to me, my turn to answer the question.

"Mashed potatoes. It's the only thing I know how to cook, but I do a pretty good job."

We bounce off more questions, the surface of our lives echoing off the walls, not caring who if anyone could hear us anymore; the cathedral seemed empty but there were plenty of corners to hide in. My laughter feels strange as we continue—this odd thing traveling out of me—effortlessly given up to the night. In a way, I almost don't recognize it when it echoes back to me.

There is a moment of quiet, and I roll onto my back to stare at the stained-glass saints and Jesus depicting several scenes from the Bible my bad Catholic self can't identify; my wings crunch under my weight, and I shift until I am comfortable. The quiet is only interrupted by moments of incredulity from Miles's responses to my questions.

"What do you mean you haven't seen *The Princess Bride*?" I pop up from where I was lying on my pew and drape my hand over the backrest to slap him on the shoulder.

Miles holds his hands up. "Don't hurt me, it won't change the fact that I haven't seen it."

"Inconceivable," I reply.

"Not really, just not a lot of time for movies."

"Inconceivable!"

"You keep using that word," Miles says, and I wait for him to complete the line as surely this is a jest. But he doesn't.

I finish it for him, "I don't think it means what you think it means."

"I'm pretty sure I do know what it means."

"Whoa, you don't even get the reference." I shake my head—how could there be a person on earth who hasn't seen that film? They must have shown it fifty times on TV during the summer Adam left. I knew it by heart. "Do you have a favorite film then? Oh God, it's *Scarface*, isn't it? Why is it always *Scarface*?"

"It is not *Scarface*." He hops up on the bench, walking along its length. I watch him, high above me. "Okay, so growing up we all want to be like our parents at one point, right?"

"Right. My mom had these amazing bangs when I was nine, so I totally grabbed a pair of scissors and—" I mimic cutting my own hair.

He stretches his long legs, hopping over on my pew and sitting on top of the backrest. "I bet you looked amazing."

"I thought I did."

"How did your mom take it?"

She grounded me. And Adam, who was supposed to be watching over me but was playing video games instead. "Not well."

For a moment I fear bringing up that memory will cause the others to tumble through. I am ready to shove them back by force if necessary.

Miles leans down, grabbing a long strand of hair that's come loose from my ponytail, and I forget all about the threat of the past. "You were saying about wanting to be like our parents . . ."

He drops the strand and hops down beside me. "My dad was, is, a huge Eddie Murphy fan. So I wanted to be a huge Eddie Murphy fan too. Watched all his films religiously, even the bad ones."

"So," I interrupt, "it's *Coming to America* or *Trading Places*."

Miles narrows his eyes, looking me up and down as if assessing me for the first time.

"What? Surprised I know my eighties comedy?"

"I will never underestimate you again." He touches my nose, a quick tap before he continues on. The gesture—one of familiarity and amusement, lightens my heart. I try and look away to the stained glass or the wrought-iron lamps that hang just above our heads, but I can't keep my eyes away from him for too long. "It should be one of those, but no. The damn film I always go back to is *The Golden Child*." He cringes as he says it.

"I don't think I've heard of that one."

He exhales. "Don't do it, it's horrible. Eddie Murphy is a private detective who has to find this chosen kid before a lot of demons do. It's wrong in so many ways. It's so bad."

"Then why is—"

"I have no idea. I think it's so bad it's good in a way. We watch it to make fun of it and it's amazing. Truly. Horrible but amazing."

"I believe that's called a guilty pleasure, and there is no shame in that."

"Care to name one then?"

Well, I walked right into that one. My face is turning beet red as I make a mental list of all my guilty pleasures: Marathoning *Teen Wolf* on repeat until I can recite each line by heart. The artistic readings of the tattered romance novels Em and Kara take home from the library. Actually that might be a good one to share.

"It's not really a guilty pleasure as much as an artistic performance," I start.

Miles nods. "You're stalling."

"I am."

He takes my hand in his. "Trust me. Whatever it is, it can't be worse than *The Golden Child*."

"Sometimes my friends and I borrow these really steamy romance novels from the library and then read them aloud like a play."

He's trying not to laugh. "Like trashy story time?"

I hide my face in my hands. "Yes."

He pulls my hands down, trying to meet my eyes. "Put me down for Tuesdays."

"Will do." I imagine him in my bedroom reading the silly lines from the really old romance novels and I almost start cracking up, until the image becomes just him and I, alone on my bed, novel on the floor . . . *oh God, don't blush, don't blush. Look at something calming. There's Jesus, oh good. That's working.*

We are quiet again, another lull—they get easier each time. Miles starts tapping on the back of the pew, a simple rhythm at first, then a beat. Each finger taps out a different note. I watch the rapid movement, transfixed. A song is forming. He starts to hum, closing his eyes, and I take the opportunity to stare at him without him looking back; his body is so relaxed, the muscles in his arms pulsing, his other hand resting on his thigh, I want to reach forward and lace our fingers together. I want to rest my hand on his thigh.

"Who's there?" The voice bounces off the walls as a figure comes into view. Miles and I dive between the pews. He can't see us. Miles pulls down his banjo; we huddle and wait. I inch closer, relishing the brush of his breath against my neck. The footsteps get closer. "Who is there?"

His eyes meet mine—he is a breath away. *Close the gap, close the gap, close the gap.* "Run?"

I nod. "Run." And we bolt, not waiting for the steps to get any closer.

"There are no shenanigans allowed on sacred ground," the guy, whoever he is, calls after us, but we're already back into the night, in the streets, music folding around us, welcoming us in.

We slow after two blocks, our hands still entwined.

Miles tsks at me. "Now, now, Sunshine. No shenanigans allowed."

"Wouldn't dream of it."

"Which way?" he says.

I smile and tuck my hands over my chest. "Ready?"

His gaze flicks down to my waist, to where his hands would soon be. "Ready."

I close my eyes, mouth quirking, and spin.

When he stops me my hand hits his side, I lose my balance and fall toward him. My eyes fly open and the first thing I see is his mouth inches from me, his hands warm along my hips. I point somewhere off in the distance behind him.

He holds me for a moment before we break apart.

When I speak my voice is light and does not tremble. "I'll miss our little sanctuary. Won't you?"

Miles looks back at the cathedral, then back to me. "Sanctuary is a person, not a place."

Sound of Silence

As the days passed, I experienced a level of quiet from Adam that I hadn't known before. Not that my brother had ever been loud, but he was always accompanied by sound: the music he played in his room, the laughter from his friends, the general clumsiness of his movements through the house, an overall disregard for noise levels in his daily life.

When Adam left for duty it was the quiet that was most unsettling—an entire life, a space usually occupied now vacant and gaping—the quiet multiplied and invaded all the spaces he used to live in. As much as I tried I could not re-create the soundtrack that was my brother and I did not want to—his absence should be felt, as if somehow we kept him safe by missing him.

Eventually we got used to it, his noise becoming a memory and the absence of him becoming the reality to the point that when Adam returned I didn't notice right away that the old noise hadn't come with him. Often I would look up from my homework or reading and find Adam standing by the door, staring, before he turned away and went to his room like he hadn't been there at all.

AND AS MY brother muted, those around him insisted on filling the void: my parents, his friends, strangers in church—one-sided conversations that canceled out the gaps he left behind.

Maybe that's why it took me so long to see the shifts, the differences, the brand-new soundtrack . . . because everyone else was so damn loud.

THE SUNDAY AFTER my brother left his room for the first time during the day was an exciting one for my mother. It signaled to her that Adam was ready to enter the world, which she couldn't wait for him to do. We would attend church as a family, and we'd finally get to sit with Adam in public where everyone would see what a miracle he was.

After Mass everyone shook Adam's hand and patted him on the back, thanking him for his service. To one person after another, Adam nodded and offered a thin-lipped smile. When I was ten my mom gifted me an *Emily Post's Etiquette* book for Christmas; I never read it, but I wonder if there was a section on this sort of situation . . . perhaps a whole chapter called "On Giving Thanks for Military Service" or something.

Tavis was there. He came over, giving Adam the most awkward hug, telling him how good it was to see him and how they should hang out again soon even though the last time they'd hung out had been in kindergarten. He'd pulled me into a hug before I was able turn away. Tavis and his family have been going to this church for years, and as the neighborhood started becoming more diverse, more and more Latinos joined the congregation. Now Father Lopez slipped into Spanish with every other sentence. Tavis's family didn't seem to mind and continued to attend.

WE TOOK OUR seats closer to the front than we usually did, the crowd parting to let us through. When the service started Father Lopez acknowledged my brother's return, *Le damos las gracias al Señor,* thanking God for his safekeeping and that of other loved ones also returned. My mother squeezed my brother's arm, then looped hers around my father's.

I hadn't seen my parents this happy in a while, it was amazing to see that full-watt smile again—for so long it was just a ghost, a crescent moon. My brother kept his gaze down, staring at the faint scratches and dents in the back of the wooden bench in front of us. Despite his silence, having him physically sitting right next to me felt like a miracle. When Father Lopez asked us to rise to recite the peace at the end of the service, I noticed the fresh line carved into the wood where Adam sat, the dark stain under his thumb.

After the service my brother gave my mother a kiss on the cheek and left with old friends. He arrived home hours later, smelling of beer, knocking on my door.

"What are you doing?"

I held up my book. "Knitting." It was amazing how I felt like a child then, glowing because my brother was paying attention to me, simultaneously thrilled and afraid that at any moment I might say the wrong thing that would make him go away.

Adam nodded and slumped down on the bed, my stuffed unicorn, Mr. Pointy, crashing down on the floor. I tucked a blanket over him, slamming into the rank smell of beer. I swatted at it like a fly.

"Tired?"

"All the damn time."

Tall, Dark Strangers and Louisiana Vampires

I HAVE LEARNED MANY THINGS ABOUT NEW ORLEANS IN THE last thirty minutes. First is that streetcars are quite fun, but only when they aren't full of very drunk, very grabby people. Although being shoved up against Miles during the course of our ride was not too shabby. And second, if Miles is right he won't let you forget it.

"Okay," I shout out into the night. "Once again, you were a hundred percent correct about the streetcar."

"I'm sorry." He places his hand against his ear. "I did not hear you. What was that again?"

I hop down the street ahead of him, then turn, walking backward while still facing him, and say, "Miles was right! Miles was right! I will trust him in all things."

"That's all I ask." He catches up.

"I just wanted to do something New Orleansy."

"I understand," he says, looping his arm around mine. "And I know I'm not supposed to be planning or strategizing, but there happens to be a New Orleans institution just round the corner."

"Really? What is it?"

He shrugs. "I think we need another sugary pick-me-up. Don't you?"

CAFÉ DU MONDE is sprinkled—no, not sprinkled, it's *swimming* in powdered sugar. The chairs, the floors, the customers all dusted in the same sweet sugar as the confections they produce. Miles and I wait in line with other fairies and demons of the night until it's our time to order, watching tray after tray of beignets coming out of the kitchen topped with mountains of delicate powder, so much that I can't even see the beignet underneath. There might not even be any, just a plate of powdered sugar ready to be whisked away by the breeze, sweetening the air around us.

There's still a bustle in the Quarter. It is noticeably quieter than the parade route in the sense that we no longer have to shout in order to hear each other, but it is by no means silent. Pockets of music tumble out of bars and conversations between friends hover in the air.

When we reach the window our order is waiting for us.

Miles gives the young girl behind the counter a quick hug before we scoop up the treats.

"Friend?"

"Sort of. Been giving her free guitar lessons in exchange for food. Not bad, right?"

I peek into the bag. It's piping hot and the beignets smell amazing. And even though I've already eaten my fill today, there is always room for more beignets. Bloody hell. It's still warm from the fryer, and the heat helps melt the sugar on my tongue. We walk and talk, licking sugar off our fingers. For a moment I fantasize about licking the flakes of powdered sugar that stick to the side of his lips. I sip at the hella strong chicory coffee and pass it back to Miles, watching as his lips touch where mine once were. The coffee is bitter on my tongue despite the shot of warm milk and sugar.

We stop by a statue of a man on a horse that is nowhere near as interesting as Miles's lips, but I pretend that it is. "Are we in Jackson Square?"

"Well, look who read the brochure!" Miles jokes, but he's pretty much right. Before we came to New Orleans I wrote down a list of places I wanted to see (Kara and Em would be so proud if they knew), and Jackson Square was one of them. The little square looks as lovely as the pictures online, the glow from the lamplights in the night giving it a particularly romantic tone.

Miles pulls me over toward a relatively quiet corner away from the tarot card readers and opposite what appears to be a store dedicated completely to Tabasco sauce. "Really?"

He passes the coffee back and Miles follows my line of sight and laughs. "Yeah, it's pretty popular. Normally this wouldn't be a great place to park, but most people are still up in Carrollton and Oak or over on Bourbon Street, and other touristy stops."

"Jackson Square isn't touristy?"

"Not during Mid-Summer."

Looking around, there are still quite a few people in the square, but I can breathe and feel like the air is my own instead of sharing with my neighbor. We pass the café au lait until we drain the last drop. Tossing our garbage in a nearby bin.

The cathedral in Jackson Square is much smaller than the one at Loyola. Three towers reach out to the sky over its white facade.

"It's beautiful," I say to no one in particular.

"And haunted," Miles says.

"Really?" I turn and come face-to-face with Miles, who has moved closer to me without my noticing. The lamplight bounces off his eyes, pulling out the hints of gold hidden within. "Granted, most places in New Orleans are."

"Really?" I mentally remind myself to expand my vocabulary.

"A couple of fires, hurricanes, and the yellow fever equal a ghost in every corner." He leans in close, and I lighten at the familiarity of his body language. It's amazing how Miles makes me feel like I've known him forever. "Even a vampire or two."

I laugh, feeling the warmth of Miles's proximity bubble through my body. "Vampires?"

Miles swings around a post, reminding me of an old Fred Astaire movie my dad watched not long ago. He stops inches from my face. His eyes flick down to my lips then back up to my eyes. "We got everything here: vampires, ghosts, voodoo, fortune-tellers, music, food, alligators. You name it. Except maybe dry heat."

He isn't kidding. My shirt sticks to my skin as we walk, and I know from the times I spent visiting family in PR there is no amount of deodorant that can help me now. I try not to think about it too much as we continue, and the wind has been kind enough to pick up, keeping the situation from getting worse. Although I'm pretty sure my hair is a constant vortex of strands above my head.

"Even the St. Louis Cathedral has a resident ghost."

We look up at the peaks of the cathedral piercing the sky. "I didn't think you could haunt a sacred place."

"He doesn't really haunt, more like cohabitate." The way Miles is looking at the cathedral it's almost like he can see the ghost itself. "He was a friar or something— loved this place so much he just stayed even after he died. There was a fire a few years back and people say they saw his ghost running in and out of the building with the local firemen, pulling out painting after painting."

"How did they know it was him? I mean, if New Orleans has a ghost in every corner couldn't it have been your friendly neighborhood ghost?"

Expecting this, Miles continues, "It could, but you see, inside St. Louis is a painting of this particular friar, and our friendly fireman was a perfect match."

We weave through a mass of people huddled together.

"That sounds really sweet, actually."

Miles leans in conspiratorially. "They say if you are walking around in the early morning you can catch him taking his daily walk."

"Gotta keep that healthy living even when you're dead, I guess."

The Tabasco store is amazing. It's closed but we peek through the windows at all the Tabasco-branded items. My favorite is the crate of baby Tabascos with a taxidermied alligator (or is a crocodile?) sticking out of it.

"What about this place? Does the Tabasco store have a ghost or a vampire or two?"

"I don't know. Friendly ghosts stories are one thing but vampires . . . could be dangerous. They could hear me."

"I'll protect you."

"You? You got a wooden stake in that bag of yours?"

"I got a cross. Vampires hate that, right?" I pull out the small silver cross I keep tucked under my shirt. A gift from my grandmother before she passed away—so light that I often forget I'm wearing it. I always think I should switch it out for another piece of jewelry, but I never do—because of her more than anything else.

"That looks special."

I think of lying, of shrugging and moving the conversation back to surface things that will keep the thoughts at bay. But I don't.

"My abuela gave it to me," I say, and wait for the panic to rise but it doesn't come. Abuela Julia is a safe memory.

"She pass on?"

"Yeah, how did you know?"

"Tone—you can always hear it in the tone," he says, "when someone's special in your life. Good or bad. Tell me about her."

"I thought no baggage?"

"Your grandmother is part of your baggage?"

I run my fingers up and down the necklace, thoughts of her bubbling up, birthdays, talks over the phone. My eyes tear a bit, but again the darkness doesn't push through. "No."

I smile—finally something I can offer.

"All right then, tell me about her, or we can go back to Questions, Questions. I still don't know what your favorite color—"

"Blue."

"Damn, there goes at least a solid minute."

"Okay, okay. She was—great."

"Great sounds good, keep going."

I push him, he makes a show of almost falling over before straightening. As we continue on, it starts to rain like a switch has been flipped. We dash from covering to covering, avoiding the worst of the downpour.

"She was born in Puerto Rico but moved at a pretty young age to the States with my grandfather, so her main language was Spanglish, as my mom would say. She always wanted to move back permanently but never did. She went back every year to visit family and stock up on *recao* and spices, though."

We pause under a tiny red awning. The next one is farther away, and we plan our attack. "That's a pretty dry story."

I nod and think back to how my abuela Julia would recite the story like she was reading off a grocery list. "You aren't far off. She said she and my grandfather had the most boring courtship in all humanity."

We jump over a widening puddle like little children and duck under another awning. As quickly as it started the rain stops. We risk a look and lean over to peek at the sky. The rain cloud is gone but there are more off in the distance, so many that eventually we won't be able to tell the difference between them and the sky.

"I find that hard to believe. Did she love him?"

"Yes, but I think if you knew her you would understand. She was very frank and didn't really care for flowery language. Things were a simple yes or no in her life. I asked her once if she loved me."

"And?"

"She said 'of course,' but it was in such a factual way—you know? Like she had no time for oversentimentality but that didn't mean she didn't love me." I shrug, there are times I wish I could handle things the same way. "I never met my grandfather—he died before I was born—but I wonder if his side of the story was different."

"He from PR too?"

"Yeah—they met in high school, came over here together. Here being the US." It's really hard not to splash into puddles as we continue walking but I know future me will hate the wet sneakers. "So do you think the cross will do?"

Miles reaches over, playing with the necklace but being delicate at the same time. Does he notice my breathing becomes a bit shallower when his fingers graze my collarbone? "Cross is only as good as your faith, every vampire hunter knows that."

"Well then," I say. "I guess you're toast."

I try to make my tone light, but it doesn't come out that way. Still, Miles smiles and releases the cross, careful not to touch me. "We'll have to be cautious then."

"Yeah."

"So does this mean you speak Spanglish?"

"*Claro que sí.*" I beam. "One hundred percent fluent."

"I know a little bit of French, mostly food, and about ten words in Arabic that I learned to impress girls."

I laugh. "Did it work?"

"You tell me, Lila. *Anta tahbisu anfasi.*" He reaches for his hat, remembers it's gone, and tips an imaginary one toward me. "Are you impressed?"

"Erm." I pinch my thumb and index finger together. "*Un poquito,* but very little. I think you still owe me a vampire story?"

"Forgive me. Now—my details are a bit fuzzy from hearing it told by different people, with completely different versions."

"Which means you can't remember how it goes," I interject, teasing.

Miles arches a brow, picking up on my tone. "I remember the important bits."

"Mmm." A pair of cops walk by us, and a group of neon goldfish run past, tossing a pair of beads at them with a wink. One of the cops shakes his head, as he and his partner continue on.

"Our story starts in the sixteenth or seventeenth century in France."

"France?"

"*Oui.*"

Miles flips his banjo around and strums it, adding a tune to the story.

"So this man, everyone loved him, ladies wanted him,

men wanted him, etc., etc. You get the drift." As he tells his tale, Miles switches up the tune to match the words. He never looks down as he plays, confident that his fingers know what they are doing. "But like in any good story there was something off about our guy, a few things that stood out if you were paying attention—which some people were, obviously, or this story would not exist."

He changes the beat to something more soft and mysterious. "One: in the time that he was in France, around twenty years, I think, he never aged. Not even a little bit. People explained it away—I think he had some obsession with cosmetics, I don't know, but people found an excuse for his seeming fountain of youth. Like if he was around today people would say it was all due to the vegan lifestyle and avoiding sugars, right?"

"He'd be totally shooting the wheatgrass."

Miles and I sync up, our steps falling in line with each other, echoing on the cobblestones.

"Exactly. So that's one, then two: no one ever saw him eat, not one bite, not ever. They only ever saw him drink."

I kicked a pebble across the street. "Liquid diet, dead giveaway."

"You'd think, but like I said, people loved him, so it all amounted to a couple of odd things, nothing major, and you could attribute all of this to rich white man eccentricities, right?"

"Right."

"But then . . ." Miles strums a few ominous chords, which would probably be scarier if not played on a banjo. "Dude dies, everyone mourns, yada, yada, yada, life goes on. Skip to New Orleans around the 1920s to another man with similar behavior. Same build, life of the party, wealthy, liquid diet."

"So?"

"So one night this dude gets a bit . . . bitey." He lunges at my neck for effect. I jump back, almost colliding with another person. I apologize before slapping Miles on the shoulder. "She escapes and gets the police—but by the time they get there he's long gone. They search his entire apartment and only find bottles and bottles of what looks like wine. What a waste, why not have a drink to . . ."

"They drank it?"

"Of course they drank it! It's Orleans, it's the 1920s Prohibition, thousands of people making homebrews, probably a horrible day at the office, moving on. When they drink the wine . . ." Miles pauses, waiting for me to interrupt. I should be annoyed, but there's a playful nature to his pause. I motion for him to continue. "They quickly spit it out. Because it wasn't just wine, of course, all the bottles were mixed with blood. And from there it's just a hop and a skip to vampire lore and so on."

"Did he ever show up again?"

"Nah. Probably made his way somewhere else if he's smart, like Jersey or New York . . ."

"Excellent story, dear bard. But I don't think that makes him a Louisiana vampire if he was born in France, right?"

"Like the French and Leo da Vinci, we like to appropriate people."

We stroll around the square, walking around the dozens of tarot readers.

"How do you know all this history?"

He shrugs. "It's a story all the tour guides tell around the city. Sometimes you'll be walking down the street and hear one story told, cross the street and hear it finished by someone else." To prove his point he gestures to a group of people two blocks away, traveling in one large mass before stopping across from the cathedral. One of them breaks away and addresses the rest. She must be the guide. "Must be a dozen or more tours happening around here at once. Not hard to wander into a tale or two."

We smile at each other for a second before we sit there by the entrance to the cathedral, watching the people move around us. Those heading to or from Oak, tourists being pulled into doorways to have their fortunes told . . . so many tall, dark strangers to encounter that I consider for a moment getting mine read.

"When I was thirteen I had my fortune told in one of those little shops that pop up by restaurants, the kind that start off with a neon sign, then carpeted stairs with giant dark stains all around." He leans in close as I talk, and I shift toward him. "I paid twenty dollars to be told that I would marry twice but only fall in love once."

"Tough news for the other guy," Miles says. "Care to try it again?"

"I'm not handing my cash to some dude who couldn't bother to change out of his stained Bermuda shorts this morning."

Miles follows my line of sight to the older gentleman sitting in a beach chair. "Bet he gives more accurate readings than all the others though. Like, maybe that's his curse, he knows the future but no one will take him seriously because of his pants."

"Why wouldn't he just change his pants?"

"He can't. Those shorts are who he is, and he must be true to himself above all."

"Maybe he's like Cassandra from the Greek myths." I take a good look at the schlubby fortune-teller, a deck of tarot cards spread out on a small foldable table in front of him. Unlike his fellow fortune-tellers, he has no sign declaring his ability. Accompanying the shorts is a palm-tree-patterned shirt worn over a sleeveless tee and sandals with socks. "He knows the truth, but no one will believe him."

"Socks and sandals can never be taken seriously."

Miles hops up. "Let's do it."

"Let's do what?"

He reaches out his hand for mine. I place my hand in his before I know what's happening. "Let's do what?"

"Let's get our fortunes told from socks and sandals. Why not?" He pulls me to my feet; I tumble into him. "We already know there's a tall, handsome stranger in your future. So maybe I can get some juicy secrets from those cards."

He keeps his tone light, but Miles's smile quickly fades into something deeper—is he remembering my reticence back in the cathedral? My heart hammers in my chest, the rise of panic. My hand is still in his, and his other is around my waist. I've made no move to push myself off, and we stand like that, entwined under the shine of the street-lamps. I slow my pulse—there will be no secrets spilled yet. Miles dips his head down, my own reaching up before I whisper, "Who says you're handsome?"

I push him away, massive grin on my face. I walk away from him, knowing he will follow.

After a moment I hear, "But I am tall, right?"

I'm with the Band.
I Am the Band.

WE LEAVE JACKSON SQUARE WITH A SPIN AND A NEW DIREC-
tion. As quiet seeps into the rest of our walk, I become
restless and just a bit worried—the memories are beginning
to creep in like water when it's quiet and I know it's so easy
to drown. I've kept my body from tensing, but I know all
my emotions are visible on my face if only for moments at
a time. Miles watches me, too kind to press, or maybe he's
just waiting for me to open up more. I need a distraction.
When a group of three women stumble out of a bar, gig-
gling down the street, the cadence of the music reaches out
into the night, tangling around me.

The night has been amazing so far, but I need another
jolt—I need my heart to beat out of my chest—I need to

feel alive if only for shorts bursts of time. I walk into the bar, not caring if Miles is behind me. It's dark and I feel the band—the thump of the bass—before I see them in the back. They're playing folk mixed with jazz, and the song keeps luring me forward. It starts: *I hardly know my name.*

There's a small dance floor—or just a bit of floor where people have moved the tables and started to sway. Under the music I can hear the chatter of the people around me talking about heading out, but nothing can drown out the beat. *I grievin' myself away. Haven't had a bite to eat since the day before yesterday.*

I've never heard this song before, but something tells me it was written long ago—there's a sense of place and time even though the tempo feels new and energetic. My feet are ready to hop in once again when there's a hand on my shoulder, twisting me around. I turn to face a giant of a man with a hat far too small for his head. "You got ID?"

Shit.

Technically I do, but that's not going to help me out at all since it's not fake. I sputter and grasp for something to say when Miles circles around the guy and maneuvers his banjo to the front of his body, tipping his imaginary hat. "We're the next act."

"Next act?" The giant is narrowing his eyes, looking at Miles, then at the banjo, trying to figure out if this kid is for real.

"Yeah." The lies come smooth and fast. Miles strums

the banjo for effect, no care in the world. "Got a call from Mike that you could slot us in. We're really excited to perform." Miles turns to me. "It's our what . . . third show?"

I nod far too eagerly but I am so far from good at this. Which is odd because with all the lying I've been doing to myself the past few days you'd think I'd be a pro by now. Instead I stumble on the words and inch closer to Miles. "Third, yes, third."

Miles lets his charming smile shine and charges on. "Third show since we became an official band. The Midsummer Boys—'Boys' being more of a general term, like when you say 'hey guys' but there are also girls in the room, you know?"

The giant looks us over, probably taking in the blue hair, red wings, lack of any other band members, and only one instrument. If he doesn't see what bad liars we are then he is probably drunk or too tired to care. Fingers crossed for either.

Finally he says, "Who the fuck is Mike?"

Welp.

"We just played Mid-Summer," I blurt out.

"Who ain't," he says, and we are screwed, I know we are. "There is no second act today. We got open mic on Tuesdays."

Miles has this earnest bewildered look to him now and it is golden. Give the kid an award, people. "I swear we got a call to perform."

"I heard. From Mike. Who doesn't exist. And you two don't look old enough to be in here, let alone the vicinity."

"We came all this way." Miles is pushing it. I want to tug on his sleeve and leave before this gets any worse, but I'm frozen behind him, the giant's face half in shadow, half illuminated by large swatches of blue light. "Is there any way we can go up and play?"

Uh, please no. I have no musical ability whatsoever.

"Not tonight."

I let out a breath—no one here wants to hear me sing. I don't want to hear me sing. Cats in heat would be worried for me if I started to sing.

"All right, I get it." Miles drops his shoulder, letting out a sigh. "Bummed, but we get it. Can we stick around and check out our competition?"

Giant looks to me, then back to Miles, clearly asking himself if it is even worth it to continue this conversation. He should have thrown us out long ago, and he knows it. I'm hoping for the desperation of a man who is too tired to care and longs for the comfort of a good bed. Come on, Tired.

"No drinks," he says finally. "I catch either one of you near the bar—"

Miles nods. "You got it."

"Just music."

"All we need."

The giant leaves us and we both exhale, my body sags with relief.

"I knew you were trouble," Miles says with a wink. We move closer to the band, picking out an empty table, and Miles leaves his banjo, reaching for my hand.

"Come on." He motions me toward him. "You owe me for almost getting me clobbered."

It's true, Miles totally saved my butt. I go to stand up, but my wings get caught on the chair and tug me back down.

"It's time to take these off." I reach around the back and end up almost unhooking my own bra, my face flashing crimson. "Dang, she really tacked these on good."

I scrunch up my nose and turn away from Miles, pointing at the wings. "Uh, can you?"

After a pause, I feel Miles close the gap between us. "What do—what do I do?" It's the first time he's sounded so unsure and nervous the whole night. It is strangely satisfying to fluster him.

"There's a safety pin in the middle, just unhook it."

I don't add "without unhooking my bra," but I have a feeling from the pauses in his reply that I don't have to say that out loud. I can barely feel Miles's hands as he works, his fingers like a whisper above my skin. If I lean back just a bit his mouth would be inches from my neck; I feel my body sway, getting closer without my permission, he's right there, my head reaching just past his shoulder, and force myself to straighten. After another minute I feel the release of the wings and the removal of a weight I didn't remember I was carrying.

"I've probably smacked so many people in the face with these," I say as he hands them over my shoulder, steadying before I turn.

"All part of Mid-Summer."

I drop the wings by the banjo and join Miles on the edges of the dance floor, just as the band starts playing a cover of "Come and Get Your Love" by Redbone. I feel far too conscious of where my body is positioned in comparison to Miles's until more people join us, swaying around us. Then it feels like we're all dancing together, one big mass of revelry, like it once was, and it's okay to let go.

Heyyyy, heeeyyyyy, the song says, and I reply with my hips. Miles laughs and shakes his head. Soon I lose track of him, and I'm dancing with a stranger, a woman with long dark-brown hair and a red dress that reminds me of the twirling dresses of Broadway musicals; she's wearing bright-green tights with thorns painted up her legs, accented with glitter. When she spins, she blooms, a blazing rose in the night. She's switching partners left and right; she doesn't care who she dances with as long as she dances—so we gravitate toward each other, tuned into the song and the call of the lead singer. *Heyyyy, heeeyyyyy.* I smile the kind of smile that will hurt in a minute, big and wide, pulling at my skin and tugging my muscles apart.

She and I are partners for this song and the next; people swell around us, but no matter how many twists and turns, the flash of red anchors me. I am safe with her, with this stranger, and I believe she feels safe with me. The costumes around me are coated in gallons of sequins and glitter and after each song I am coated anew with the shine of others.

I've never danced so much in my life, and it feels like in this one day I've used my body more than it's ever been used, more than it's ever lived. I sway and I move and if I look the fool, so be it. I can sense Miles near me, his energy, ever present but not controlling, finding his own way to let go. The song goes on and on, and I close my eyes and let go because everyone on the dance floor is in it together, not caring if we bump into each other or step on toes.

Snippets of conversation travel above the music, broken pieces forming a whole.

"You gonna ride it out?"

"Yeah, you?"

"Darn straight—ain't no safer place."

"Few of us gonna kick it here until it passes over. Plenty of liquor to drink. We'll be just fine."

Song turns into song, and I feel arms wrapping around my waist and drawing me near. I know they belong to Miles without opening my eyes. I let him pull me near and move with me; he holds me by the waist as I lean back, testing his strength. The music slows, and I rest my head on his shoulder. From the corner of my eye I see the woman in red with her own partner; she catches me watching and smiles before she disappears. Miles wraps one arm tighter around my waist, the other across my back, sliding it up my arm to hold on to my hand. I feel my back tingling as we stay that way for more than one song; fast or slow, it doesn't matter, we are constant in each other.

Miles's breath is on my shoulder, his hand firm at my back. I am flush up against him, and it feels like the heat of the Louisiana sun courses through us. But as close as we are, we could get closer, I want to get closer. We need to get closer, and it scares me. Terrifies me. Enough to stop me from pushing this further, but not enough to pull me back, away, from him.

How can you want so much in so little time?

I shut my eyes again and let the thoughts just roam: Miles kissing me. Miles running his hands down my body, settling on my lower back just above my bare skin—I tense. As if he sees what I'm thinking, Miles dips his head down to my neck and lays a soft kiss along my skin. Then another.

He rests his hand on my cheek. "Too much?"

"No," I lie. It is too much, and yet not enough. Miles tucks a strand of hair behind my ear and waits, his hand now just a gentle presence on my back. I tilt my head toward him, an invitation. He closes his eyes, leaning toward me, our lips almost brushing when we are jostled away from each other.

Miles shields me as two grown men tussle over who knows what.

"Time to go?" I say. Somewhere a table falls, glass breaks.

"I know just the place," he says.

The Saddest Story

"WE ARE NOT BREAKING AND ENTERING," I SAY OUT INTO THE night, but only loud enough for Miles to hear. When we left the club I swore we'd continue our almost-kiss out on the cobblestone streets, but instead Miles tugs me along with the promise of someplace special. Something to wait for. I think of tossing the wings, frayed from all the excitement of the day, a gash on one side, ripped tape on the other. But still, I hold on tight, deciding against throwing them out; they too would survive the night with me, even if at the end all that remained was a bit of red cellophane and wire.

"Who said anything about breaking and entering? I said I know a place."

"No, you said, 'I know a place but no one might be

home, not that it matters,' to be exact. Hence breaking and entering and misdemeanor felony or whatever."

"Okay . . . I phrased that incorrectly, I accept that, but how much *Law & Order* do you watch?"

"Not enough to get us out of trouble when we're caught." I lower my voice, afraid of attracting too much attention from the people around us, which is silly now that I think about it because everything attracts too much attention on Mid-Summer and so nothing does. You could scream "I am a golden god" from a rooftop and no one would notice. Someone might throw you a necklace, but that's about it. I skip a few steps to land next to Miles. "And if it wasn't very clear from my scintillating conversation with that bouncer, I am a terrible liar."

"Oh, that was pretty clear—like, crystal clear—but I'm not asking you to lie or break and enter anywhere, Lila. Just trust me."

He snags my hand again, bringing it to his lips, eyes so intent on mine. His kiss is electric, shock traveling across my skin. "I haven't led you down the wrong path yet, have I?"

"No, I guess not." But there's a first time for everything.

We're back in the Quarter, weaving through more costumes—it's impressive how many people New Orleans attracts during a celebration. I wonder if during the regular February Mardi Gras you're just confined to the same block for hours because you can't move anywhere.

As we move I hear pockets of conversation around me. Miles is right, there are at least three midnight ghost tours happening at the same time. I leave the story of the Louisiana vampire on one corner and pick it up at the next. We pass an imposing white marble building that emanates light from every window; inside there's a large group entering the lobby of what I now see is a hotel—historic from the looks of it. I pause by the entrance, trying to listen to the story, curious if the guide is any better at telling it than Miles.

"Now right above this lobby"—the tour guide is an older man, white hair and mustache, cap embroidered with Something-Something City Walk Tours; he motions with his thumb at the floor above him—"is a grand ballroom. Marble floors, chandeliers, grand piano. You can just imagine the parties they threw there, folks, real ragers."

He laughs at his own joke even though no one else does. The tour guide is trying *hard* not to lose his audience, but he lacks the oratorical magic to keep them riveted. I feel Miles come up to stand behind me. "You cheating on me, Sunshine?"

I smirk but don't turn to face him. "Just checking out the competition."

A few people from the group have wandered away from the guide, touching the gleaming marble pillars.

"Do you think someone dusts all this or that it stays that blinding from people running their fingers over every surface—like bits of statues that shine brighter despite the time?"

"Little bit of both, I think."

The marble pillars extend all the way up to the—what? Thirty-foot ceiling? God, I pity whoever has to climb up on that ladder to dust.

The guide wrangles back his people from where they've scattered around the lobby. How many times do tours come through here? There's no gift shop to speak of, and a hotel this fancy must not be that happy with nonpaying customers traipsing around. Yet the people at the counters only offer smiles and the doorman has yet to send us on our way.

The guide starts up again. "Now you hear a lot of stories about haunted hotels, and New Orleans is home to over ten haunted hotels of note—this being one of them. As mentioned, above us stands a grand ballroom—which we can't enter, sorry about that, folks, but the kindness of this hotel only goes so far—with a very sweet occupant: a lone girl. She always appears at night, dancing under the chandelier like the party never ends."

The guide claps his hands together, making me jump and Miles snort. I swat at him without turning around. The guide points his shuffling audience to the bathrooms, asking them to meet back at the lobby in ten for the final stop.

"He didn't say anything about how she died."

"They don't know," Miles says, "or at least I've never heard the story." He bumps me with his hip, motioning me to follow. As we head out into the night, I hug my arms around myself, the air much colder now than before. The breeze picks up as we go along. I think back to my earlier conversation with Taj and Danny and wonder how far the storm is and if our night will be cut short. I don't bring it up, and maybe that means it won't actually happen.

"Shall we make up a story?" Miles says.

"What?"

"For the chandelier girl. We should make her a story."

"Yeah." The wind tosses my hair around. I rearrange my ponytail and move closer to Miles as the street narrows. "We should give her a name—a name and a story. You're the storyteller, what do you think?"

"Oh no, I'm taking a break. Union rules." Miles tugs at my arms, signaling a turn. I still have no idea where we are going, but at this point it feels natural to trust him. "It's your turn."

"No fair!"

He lifts his hands and shrugs. "Life isn't fair."

My shoulders hunch, I tense. It isn't fair. I know this. I'm knee-deep in memories, wading through them.

"Sunshine?" Miles looks worried and walks back to me, which makes me realize I stopped dead in my tracks.

"Sorry." I plaster on a smile so fake it hurts. "Just gathering my thoughts."

Miles doesn't buy it. "You sure? You looked like, like I hit a nerve or something."

I shake my head, taking the lead and pulling him down the street. "I'm fine. Let's talk ghosts. Every ghost needs a name, right?" I plunge right in. The name pops into my head. "Grace."

"Grace?" Miles tilts his head.

"Yes." I think of Grace—who was she? How old? Sixteen, I decide, like me, like Annalise. I invest in the story, let it invade my thoughts. She's at a ballroom in a hotel, so perhaps her family is traveling or came to an event? She loved to dance—enough to repeat it forever.

I think of all the stories, the myths and legends, I've devoured over the years, bookmarked and tucked away ready to be savored. Greek, Irish, African, Native American. So many tales weave together, the annoyingly tragic surfacing first, latching onto my own tale.

A young girl hurt. A young man in pain.

Annalise and Adam tumbling together to form one person made of bits from each.

I can see her in my mind: small for sixteen, a curtain of black hair, olive skin, hands that fidgeted when she thought she wasn't being watched.

"She had a heart condition," I start. I can feel Miles looking at me, his gaze a pinpoint of heat on my skin. "She was born with the condition; she wasn't supposed to dance, her heart wasn't strong enough, but she did it anyway, always in secret. To her parents she was the dutiful child, but alone . . . alone she pliéd, she practiced her port de bras, she tilted and fell and mirrored the poses she saw in her books." I twirl around on lampposts and plié on cobblestones to emphasize my point, imagining myself in my room, scanning over books. When I lose my balance Miles's hand settles on my hip until both my feet are on solid ground. "Always in secret . . . though sometimes she was wicked and when her mother or father were turned away from her she would pirouette or sway to the music in her head for a brief second before they turned around again."

I take a moment to gather my thoughts. The night is much quieter now, still, as if it held its breath waiting for me to continue.

The wind picks up again, the sky painted with clouds. I wait for rain, ready to dart beneath the nearest awning for safety, but it doesn't come. Not yet. The storm is getting closer, and I hope it doesn't take the night away with it.

"We're almost there—don't leave me hanging." Miles wraps one arm around me, banishing the cold like the day pushing away a nightmare.

"Her sixteenth birthday was a miracle. Her heart should've given out long before then, so her parents decided to throw her a lavish party. They rent the ballroom for the night and invite all of New Orleans to toast their daughter. Most important—they give her a gift." I settle closer to Miles, my body thanking me. "A dark-blue box tied with a velvet ribbon. Inside was a pair of red dance shoes and a dress to match. When she entered the ballroom her father reached for her hand and led her out to the dance floor."

Miles gathers me in his arms, and we dance down the block like in the old timey movies with curtsies and stuffy shirts. "And as her father gave her one final twirl"—Miles twirls and then dips me—"her heart gave out, and she died."

It's an odd thing, seeing the image so clearly, her father holding her in his arms, realization blooming on his face— I think suddenly of Annalise, of how her father must have held her, of Adam begging for help. I shake my head, releasing the memory, and let it fall away into the night.

Miles pulls me back up, silent, a frown across his brow.

"What?" I say.

"That is the saddest story."

I clear my throat. "Life is sad," I say.

"Not always," he replies, his voice soft.

"Sometimes," I say as he tucks a strand behind my ear. "Sometimes it is."

Sleep no more

IT'S SO ODD WHENEVER YOU ARE SPEAKING ABOUT A PERSON how much one thing contradicts another. Adam was quiet, yes, different from the person we knew before, yes, but still I feel there was a sound I would use to describe him anyway, a static building over time.

I look back at my parents during this time and there was such a careful nature about them, each question, each action punctuated by a feeling of hope. Whenever my mother asked if Adam needed anything I felt like she was under the impression that any answer was a gift because he could disappear at any moment. Same with my dad. Before, my father and Adam used to spend days fixing old crap in the garage—though they never actually completed a single project. Now my father seemed content to sit quietly while they watched a TV show or ball game—the old projects left untouched, gathering dust in the garage.

I was late to the realization that I should be happy with whatever Adam I could get and not annoy or badger him as much as I did. I was told to "let your brother be" far too many times to count. I felt like an energetic puppy constantly swatting at my brother's door, asking to be let in.

It was during this time that I would sit in church and pray to Abuela Julia, not God, who I missed every single day since she passed. I tried to channel her strength in those times, pulling whatever I could from Adam, failing as I lacked her authority. Abuela Julia would've cut through the bullshit and laid it all out for us: "Don't pretend you don't see it too, Julia."

There was no Julie or Jules with my grandmother. I was Julia always, as she was Julia always.

But if awake, Adam was quiet static; asleep Adam was not, because at night came the nightmares—or perhaps they were there during the day too, held off by the light as most nightmares are. Though . . . that feels wrong, comparing them to dreams of being chased or monsters under your bed, silly things that vanish when you open your eyes rather than what they were: constant, horrific memories beating their way forward, waiting for Adam to let them through.

So they came at night as I was falling into my own sleep and long after my parents had drifted off; I'd hear the shouts, sharp staccato sounds that burst through the night or the thump of Adam falling off his bed. The lights would flick on—a sliver under his door cutting through the darkness until daylight took its place. Sometimes I would knock on Adam's door and he'd murmur:

"Sorry, kid. Go back to sleep."

And I would sometimes, or I would hover, unsure, counting how many bumps in the night it had been this week until Adam came to the door and chased me back to my room. I would keep my door open—staring at the crack below his door until I fell asleep. Each morning my dad would ask how we'd slept, I'd shrug and Adam would lift the corners of his mouth—the perfect imitation of a smile—and say, "Not bad, you?"

Each morning I would think of channeling Abuela Julia, of slamming my hand against the table and demanding the truth, whatever it was. But I never did, and it became a routine: the quiet, the sounds, the light, the "Sorry, kid."

Until, well, until there was an until. Isn't that how it always goes?

I'M NOT SURE what was different about that night, but I didn't knock when I heard the bump, I just walked in like a fool, because what could happen? After all, this was my brother.

My Adam.

There was silence—the true silence where everything

around you has hollowed out and the only thing felt is an absence. Maybe I'd woken him up, and it wouldn't be long before the "Sorry, kid" would pop up and then we'd be back there in that damn routine, but no, there was nothing. I could see Adam still on his bed, sheets lying on the floor, twisted into a ball like he'd been punched in the gut. I froze. His muscles were taut, and I could see two scars on his upper arms that hadn't been there before he left. Those scars made me pause—had I seen them before? Had my parents? I felt the urge to shake him awake and demand the story behind them.

"Adam," I said, my voice barely above a whisper, then again, louder.

He shifted—flinched, more like it—but didn't wake.

"Adam." I inched closer, my hand hovering in midair as I reached for him. "You okay?"

My hand was on his arm for a second, maybe more, before the air whooshed out of me as I slammed down to the floor. I registered the pain before I had any time to react to it; Adam's forearm pressing down on my neck, forcing the air out of me. I couldn't breathe. I couldn't think. Words came out in small spurts. I pushed back on his chest, enough that I could speak. "STOP!" I tried to yell, but it came out as a croak, barely over a whisper. I could feel my eyes tearing up from the strain, closing, plunging me down farther into the darkness. Adam moved to shift more of his weight on top of mine, and at the back of my mind it registered that he wasn't even using his full strength, not that he needed to. Adam was at least a foot taller than me and if he shifted to place any more of his weight on mine I wouldn't be able to push him. I could tell his eyes were unfocused—he didn't even see me.

Where are you?

I thought back to our sessions—quick little lessons Adam had taught me on self-defense—but none seemed to apply to this situation, so I did what I could. I moved one leg between us, locking my knee into place, making it harder for him to use his weight against me. It hurt like hell, and my muscles stretched against his strength as he pushed my knee against my chest. I buried my nails into his skin and turned into a madwoman. I swatted. I slapped. I punched and scratched at what was basically a stone wall. "Adam, stop, STOP, it's Julie. IT'S JULIE." He grabbed my hand, then he stilled, head falling just a bit before his eyes blinked back from wherever he was. Whenever he was.

"Adam," I repeated, air finally filling my lungs. "It's Jules. Adam, please, it's Jules."

So much blinking. He took in his room, his surroundings, his arm pressing on my neck. He snapped away from me. "Jules," he said, and shifted off, slumping down by his bed, head in his hands.

"What happened?" I moved away from him and I know he saw, but I couldn't, I couldn't be that close to him in case . . .

"Nothing," he spoke into his hands. "Nothing, I just . . . I just had a bad dream."

"A bad dream?"

Bullshit—so much bullshit, but I didn't have the strength to fight him on this, and I wasn't sure the words would come out anyway.

"I get them sometimes. You shouldn't wake me like that again." He spoke to the floor, never looking up, never meeting my eyes. "It's dangerous."

"You scared me a bit."

You scared me a lot.

"I'm sorry." He looked up then, and my heart shattered. His eyes were wide and alert, filling with tears. He used the heel of his hand to wipe the tears. "I—" he started, and then cut himself off. "I'm fine. It was just a dream."

We sat in silence, my neck throbbing, Adam holding himself like he would break. He stood up finally and sat at the edge of his bed, his back to me. He said nothing, but I could see it in the slump of his shoulders and the deep breaths, the "Sorry, kid. Go back to sleep."

So I stood and left.

"Jules?"

I turned, but he still faced away from me.

"Yeah?"

"Don't . . . don't come in here when I'm like that, okay?"

"But—"

"I'll be fine—just don't come in, okay?"

I stared at Adam's back, slumped over, waiting.

"Okay, Jules?" He reminded me of something just then, of Atlas, a myth we had learned in school. Atlas was a Titan who stood against the Olympians in a great war, and when his side lost, his punishment was to hold up the sky forever.

It had nothing to do with Adam's size, but the shape of his shoulders and how if you looked at him from just the right angle you would see the curve of the celestial sphere as it lay across his back.

"Okay," I said.

Even though it felt wrong, felt like I had failed at something, I shut my eyes. I shut my eyes to Adam and closed the door.

"I'm sorry," he said again as I left him.

I stood by that bloody door for what felt like forever, not understanding, waiting to wake up, sure that this was all a nightmare; just a horrible dream caused by eating way too much ice cream before going to sleep.

My parents' door was still shut, and I wondered how they hadn't heard anything. When I got closer I could hear the mechanical sounds of a rainforest pouring from their bedroom door, blocking us out. It was all I could take—I shut myself in my room as the tears bubbled up and out; I pressed my face up against my pillows, drowning out the sound for Adam, so he wouldn't know. This was important for some reason, that Adam not hear me cry.

Exhausted, I let sleep take me over.

In the morning I stared at myself in the mirror, searching for any marks or bruises. They were faint, but my skin felt tender at the touch. I wrapped a scarf around my neck, feeling safer with it on.

At the table neither Adam nor I tried to make any eye contact. And when my father asked us how we slept, I answered, "Not bad, you?" before Adam could.

Come and Get Your Love

I CAN FEEL THE BUILDUP IN THE NIGHT. I'M NOT SURE HOW FAR the storm is now, but it can't be long—maybe an hour or two?—before we will need to end the night. I remember Abuela Julia said she could always tell a hurricane was close by how painful the wind and rain hit against your skin.

"Where are we?" The building in front of us is a lovely shade of blue that is the exact color of the sky in the daytime; it is adorned with intricate latticework all along the facade. There is a tiny little plaque by the entrance declaring the building a "boutique hotel."

"Is this place also haunted?"

"Not that I know of."

"Then why are we here?"

"Cooling off."

"A decision you probably made before the temperature dropped, I'm assuming?"

"Pretty much. But I think you'll still like it." He leads me around the building, through the back to a gate.

"Are we?"

"We are NOT breaking and entering." On the side wall there is a panel. Miles punches in a code and the panel pops open, revealing a set of keys. Taking one out, he closes the panel back up and opens the gate door. "See?"

"How did you? Is this your—"

"My house? No—like it says on the front, it's a hotel. I work here sometimes. The pay is next to nothing, but they give you perks."

"Like all the chocolate mints you can eat?"

"Like this." Miles flicks a switch somewhere and reveals a pool nestled in a bed of foliage, its size a perfect companion to the tiny hotel. "Nice, right?"

Very. Despite the temperature drop I'm still sticky and sweaty from the day and the thought of dipping into the bright-blue water is very enticing. I look up at the windows— all dark—and back to Miles. "Are there any people here?"

I don't feel like giving anyone a show even if we are allowed to be in the backyard. Miles follows my gaze. "It's closed for some renovations. They'll be open later in the year—Taj and I come around to clean the pool for extra cash, take dips in return. It's totally legit, I promise—I wouldn't ruin this night by getting you in trouble. Scout's honor."

"You were a Scout?"

"Yep, Danny and I—only for a couple of years, though. Still counts."

I've always loved the way a pool glows in the night as if every drop of water were starlight. When I was little I would hold the water in my hand, trying to catch the light with it. It didn't happen, obviously, but then Abuela Julia told me of water that does glow in beaches all over the world.

"Bioluminescent bays."

"Hmm? What did you say?"

I'd spoken out loud without realizing it. "It reminds me of these bodies of water my abuela told me about. Bioluminescent bays, caused by tiny ocean plankton, little creatures that turn water into light . . . well, the glow is theirs, of course, but I like the thought of both the plankton and the water working together, illuminating the dark. There is one in Puerto Rico even. She'd never been, but she'd always speak about it with great pride. I told her I would take her back one day and we would dip our hands in and hold the light together."

"Did you? Take her back."

"No. Didn't get a chance."

She'd passed away before I was able to. Miles seems to catch this from my voice; his reply is a soft, "Sorry."

I drop my wings on a lounge chair, inch toward the pool, and squat down to test the water: it's warm. I look up to Miles. "Heated?"

He nods.

Thank the gods. When I pull my hand back out and the water drips down, I close my eyes and imagine the bays as black as night until each creature lights up like a star or will-o'-the-wisp, luring you away to an adventure. There must have been water around the edge because as I come back up, my sneakers slip and I fall toward the pool. Miles grabs my hand, and we are suspended in the moment. I know even if I let go, he will still hold, still keep me from falling.

I pull myself toward Miles, regaining my balance, my hand still in his. "Shall we?" he says, motioning to the pool.

The realization that Miles would have to see my underwear in order for me to get in the pool hits me again. "I don't—" I say, motioning to my clothing. I could dive in with my clothes on; they were still moist from the rain. . . .

He kicks off his shoes, then his socks. "Neither do I." He settles the banjo up against the wall and pulls off his shirt and jeans before I have a moment to think; he cannonballs into the pool, splashing water on me and everything in the vicinity. I tuck away the memory of Miles half naked for the future, when he pops back out of the water, shaking the excess off his hair until it looks like someone placed little diamonds all around his head. I concentrate on anything besides the droplets running down his chest, which is just toned enough to make me blush . . . guess that banjo is heavier than I thought. "You can come in fully clothed if you want."

"Uh . . ." My brain does not compute.

All I can think is water, Miles, muscles, water, eyes with the looking, why always with the looking?

"Those shrubs can't be as interesting as you're making them out to be, Lila."

My eyes snap up, and Miles is grinning. Right. I'm sure he knows the effect he has on—well, anyone, so none of this should come as a surprise. I should be annoyed, and the fact that he knows I like him and is using it against me should bother me, but this is what I want. I want to be Lila. Julie would demur and keep her clothes on, cuffing her jeans and dipping her feet in at the edge of the pool, hoping the cute boy will swim over. Lila . . . Lila tosses her bag and wings by the banjo, pulls off her shoes, socks; she looks up at the boy who waits for her in the pool, and locks eyes as she pulls off her shirt and jeans, then jumps.

The water is delicious, warm and enveloping. I open my eyes when I hit the bottom, looking up at the world painted above me, then back to the figure of Miles waiting for me to surface. I stay down below for as long as I can, suspended in time—pushing the limits of my lungs until they burn. I close my eyes and float up to the present, the water carrying me back into to the world, unable to hide me forever. I break the surface, the chill of the night meeting me again and Miles swims toward me.

"Okay?"

I grin and splash in response. Soon we're engaging in

an all-out water war, with Miles diving under the water to tug my legs—when he comes up he is inches from my face. His gaze travels down, reminding me I'm wearing nothing but my underwear, as is he. He's so close I could kiss him by accident, just by letting the water carry me forward. A droplet hangs from his bottom lip before he licks it off.

"So," I start. "You have a lot of talents."

He lifts his eyebrow, and the corners of his mouth lift too. *Well phrased, Jules.*

"I mean." *Backtrack, Julie, you know the way now.*

"You mean."

I extricate the foot from my mouth and continue. "You play the banjo, you give guitar lessons, you're a tour guide . . ."

"Yeah, a little bit of a Jack-of-all-trades, I guess."

"That's a lot, though. I feel lazy in comparison."

He shrugs, turning away from me to float on his own. I realize I've broken our no-baggage rule; I must have, to merit this distance, particularly since—so far—Miles hasn't felt like the distance type. I'm gutted, the separation feels wrong, but I drop back, letting my legs float up, the water coming around me till I hear the echo of my heart.

"My parents are divorced."

I bring my head back up, wonder if I should say "I'm sorry" or not.

As if he hears my thought, he says, "It happened when I was six, so I've had a lot of time to deal with it."

"How did you—"

"People always say they're sorry, like they broke up the marriage or something. There really should be another way to respond, not sure what. But thank you anyway." His hand latches onto mine. We float away from each other, small waves pushing us as we hold strong. "My dad and my mom just weren't in love with each other after a while. They'd seen too many people hang on when they should've let go, so they decided not to be that way. They divorced, and my dad moved to Chicago, met someone else, and married. I have a half sister who is already on her way to becoming the world's youngest doctor."

There's a flat affect to his voice that I'm not expecting, like too many people have asked this question too many times and he's rehearsed his answer to give them the response they want. I don't want to be one of those people. I want the deep dark secrets. I pause and realize, *I want the baggage.*

"Your mom?"

"My mom stayed here. She grew up in New Orleans—everything about this city is etched into her DNA—there was no way she was gonna leave. She took her love for New Orleans into her job working for the tourism board."

"No wonder you know so much."

He nods. Then his tone changes, returning to the old Miles. When he speaks it reminds me of how my dad used to talk about Adam—with pride. "She liked rehearsing with me and the boys. We would pretend to take ghost tours and tours of the cemeteries and fancy plantations, always trying to stump her with our questions, but we never could. Things were going great for us for a while, then hurricanes hit, one after the other, closed things down for a bit. And we—she—had to carve into her savings to pay the mortgage and fix the damage to the house."

I hear his head lift out of the water as he kicks away from the edge. We collide a bit before settling back into the calm. "Not that I knew what a mortgage was at the time. My dad helped where he could, but he has a new family to take care of as well, so I started getting odd jobs when I was old enough—anything and everything they'd let a kid pretending to be older than he was do. That's the short version, I guess."

There are so many questions running through my mind, but I force myself to go back to the beginning.

"Were you angry at your parents?"

"For divorcing?"

"Yeah, and—" I test out the words in my mind before saying them out loud, hoping they come out right. "Seems like you helped a lot—and are still helping out a lot—when you should've just been a kid."

"I was a kid." His hand slips away, I press mine against my side. *Crap, I screwed this up.* His voice is not so certain as he continues. "At least I think I was." He dips under the water and comes back up again. "I don't know, I don't look back a lot. When I do things are all jumbled, like it all just happened."

I nod, knowing what he means. We were happy a moment ago, my family and I. How hard is it to go back to that moment, that second, when it feels so close?

He continues, "I close my eyes, and I can see the first job that I took and my second." He shakes his head, little drops scattering into the pool causing the slightest ripples. I'm crouching as I watch him, hiding my body in the water.

"I don't want to be an asshole," he says. "I feel like one every time I—"

"Every time you think about yourself before your family."

I smile when he looks over, relief in his eyes.

"Every time you want to complain and put yourself first." I focus on the waves, the gentle lapping of the water caused by the breeze. "The guilt is a bitch."

"Remember when Taj said I had everything figured out? I don't." He quiets. "I think I do, but I don't. Sure, I'm working toward graduating early so I can help my mom. Got a job lined up and everything. I'm thinking, it's only going to be a few years, just a few years and that's it. Then we'll be fine."

I inch closer.

"But it hasn't been fine. And I keep putting my music away for another year because I'll be an asshole if I don't. And in the end, what's another year if you really love something, because it will always be there waiting for when some time magically pops up." He cups my cheek and leans his forehead against mine. "Never does, though."

We both float again, the chill battling with the warmth of the water beneath us, watching the clouds cover the sky, like they were tucking it in to sleep. Miles doesn't ask when I felt like an asshole. I'm grateful to hold those memories off for a little while longer. I'm not ready to admit that I hadn't stopped feeling like one until tonight.

We drift like this, occasionally breaking apart, coming back together by a tug; planets in each other's orbit, periods of silence broken up by words. "Do you see your dad often?"

"We talk a lot. He plays as well, so we share lyrics and talk sets; we try and see each other once a year if we can. Doesn't always go as planned."

Miles is so free with his words, his past, even the parts that might hurt are offered up to the night, to me. Meanwhile my past catches at the back of my throat, unsure if it will emerge as a jumble or a cry, or whether it will surface at all.

"Do you get along with your half sister?"

"I'm the quintessential big brother who lives miles away. We mostly text and on occasion write outdated letters to each other."

The wind picks up, jostling the water, reminding me our time will soon be over. I ignore it.

"Like paper letters?"

"That's the one. It's really my father's fault. 'Letter writing is a motherfucking art, Miles,' he likes to say, followed by, 'Don't tell your mother that last part.' Of course he's my father, so I believed him and it turned out to be true, letter writing is an art. So sometimes I'll get an odd letter from Astrid, that's her name. I'll get this letter about the randomest crap like she had a fight with her friend and saw a movie yesterday. Letter will be dated four weeks before it's actually postdated, so by the time I get it it's old news, but I still like getting them."

"I'll keep that in mind." I reach my hand out, a strange automatic gesture for such a short period of knowing someone, but it feels natural.

I hook his pinkie to mine as we float. Miles is humming a tune I don't recognize, and I wonder if he just came up with it. "What is that?"

"What's what?"

"What are you humming?"

"A tune," Miles says, and I can tell that he's smiling from the tone of his voice; I even know it's a stupid smile too, the kind you make when you're being a smartass.

I forge on. "That's useful. I mean, what song is it?"

"Not sure, started as one thing and turned into another. And now it's a new thing—not sure what it is yet."

"Hum it again."

He starts and stops until the song is floating above us

and deep down below us in the water. I join in but very softly, only for a moment, long enough to feel part of it as well. "I like it. Are there lyrics?"

"Maybe."

He offers nothing more, and it irritates the crap out of me. He can't just stop sharing everything about his life after being so forthcoming. I refuse.

"I call Questions."

"It's called Questions, Questions. If you are going to invoke it, please do so correctly."

I splash water in his face, then place my hands on my hips. "Fine, I invoke Questions, Questions."

He floats away from me, a smile across his lips. "I don't think you're ready."

I dive toward him, intending to pull him under with me, but he's too fast. He jumps up and away from me, teasing. "I am too ready."

"Give it your best shot."

"All right, song writing. How do you do it? How does it happen?"

"Lots of different ways."

"Name one."

He's thinking about it.

"Once," Miles breaks the silence, "I wrote a song by pulling bits and pieces from different archives I found online."

"Like library archives?"

"Mm-hmm. Mom taught a boy how to research—proper

research—not Google and shit. It's amazing what you can find when not every other word tagged is 'penis.'"

I laugh—and it is this odd hollow thing because my ears are under the water—I wonder what he hears. I then manage to smoothly swallow a liter of pool water, coughing much of it up.

"You okay?"

I try to play it cool; I cough and fail. "Peachy. How does it work? The archives into songs."

"I would pull letters and scan journal pages and just take a sentence here and there, forming a song or a pile of crap, either/or. They don't all turn out golden; most of the time it feels like I'm trying to fit together different pieces of a puzzle that just don't work and I end up throwing away the whole thing, but once in a while . . . once in a while you get the right series of letters and it starts coming together."

"Can I hear one?"

"Maybe."

"Please?"

He smiles.

"Let's see, there's this one called 'My Darling Jean,' but you gotta imagine this with some amazing music behind it, okay?"

"Okay."

Miles clears his throat and starts; his voice is deeper than I expect.

Everything is dark here,
at night the stars are pale.
I worry about tomorrow,
because, dear Jean, what if I fail?

I shiver, his voice tangles around me, twisting around my fingers, waist, down my legs.

My heart I left with you,
the world now more than cruel
what little hope I have left
feels weak. Sometimes I think
I'll never wake and feel you
beneath me.

There's more, I can tell, but that's all Miles offers. "They sound like sad letters," I say. Yet something in his voice brought out the longing, the love and passion that linger through time.

"They were. Lots of the letters were written by soldiers during World War I, and they're all there, just scanned in and nobody knows whether the men who wrote them lived or died."

I took a deep breath, savoring the feel of Miles next to me, pretending the song is about tonight, about possibly never seeing each other again. What memories should we make? What memories did I want to make?

"How do they get the letters and not know what happened?"

"My mom says a lot of the stuff gets donated or tossed out, found in old homes. I could only tell they were from the war from the dates and a mention here or there about a battle, but not a lot, they mostly spoke about missing home and trying to hold on to the good memories."

"Good memories." I nod. Lately all the bad memories have been infecting the good ones; latching onto happy moments and simply forcing them out. I need all the good ones I can get, like tonight: tonight is a good memory.

Our pause extends, and the lapping of the waves bothers me. I close my eyes, dipping my head under; when I emerge the sky is one blanketing cloud: gray and heavy, even the quickening wind can't move it. As I stare needle-like pellets of water descend, pinpricks of cold. I let go of Miles's hand and stand, tipping my head to the side to let the water drip out. It's not painful yet, I think, we still have time.

"What are you running from, Sunshine?" he asks, his voice so soft I can't hear him at first, when I do I blank, my shoulders tense, and I freeze before I can control my body and hide my reaction.

"I'm sorry, I shouldn't have, I just thought we were—" He floats toward me, inching down so that we are level with each other.

Opening up. Sharing secrets. *We were, or more you were, Miles.*

"No baggage," Miles says, reminding himself, jumping up onto the edge of the pool.

"That's right, no baggage."

I try to sound nonchalant, like I don't want to know even more about him, like I don't think the no-baggage rule is total bull.

He dips his feet back in the water, motioning me over. I take a seat next to him but farther apart, and he moves closer until he's just a foot away, stopping short of touching me.

"Questions, Questions," he says. "But this time I want to ask something of myself."

I lift an eyebrow in response.

"I asked you what you were running from, but I should ask that of myself first, right?"

"I—I don't know, yes?" I say before continuing. "Yes. Okay. What are you running from?"

"I have a girlfriend," he says like he's ripping off a Band-Aid even though I suspected as much; a part of me imagined him with several girlfriends. He waits for my reaction.

"Was it one of the girls from the square?" I offer.

"No, actually—but they were her friends."

"And you didn't want them to see you with me in case they thought—"

Miles cut in. "I didn't want them to see me at all, regardless of whether or not you were there—no offense."

I flinch a bit, but he doesn't catch it. "Zero taken. Why didn't you want them to see you?"

"Because of Angie."

"Your girlfriend?"

"Yes."

Angie is a pretty name. I try to imagine her and Miles together, to crush these little butterflies before they grow any bigger.

"Okay." I nod, urging him to continue.

"Angie—Angela—and I have been friends since we were born. Clichéd, I know, but our mothers are best friends so we were always together. Playdates, school, same neighborhood. She's been a part of my life for so long . . . if you erased her you'd take me away too."

Miles keeps glancing at me from the corner of his eye, gauging my reaction. If he's expecting me to be jealous he's going to be waiting for a while. I should be, I suppose, I'm—okay, I'm attracted to Miles so I guess I should be threatened—but the most I feel is a brush of disappointment that I'm not the only one he's opened up to, that this wasn't 100 percent unique, just for me, but I sweep it away, reminding myself that my plan was never to jump Miles but to lose myself to the night (and maybe make out a bit). Plus the way he speaks about her, it's almost like Angie is his left leg and what would be the point of being angry at a girl he's spent his life with when I've only known him for a day?

"Eventually playdates led to date-dates and it seemed like a natural fit—dating my best friend. It's what all those movies talk about, right?"

"Right. Sounds nice."

I'm shivering, and I can't control it. I dip back down into the water before Miles can notice. I don't want to leave the pool just yet even if it's still raining.

"I guess." He shrugs.

"Are we getting to the part where this is baggage yet?" I say, and Miles splashes me hard, which makes me splash him back. He pushes me further into the water and when I try to pull him in, he holds on to my hand tight, the mood suddenly shifting. I meet his eyes, concentrating on the feel of the water around me, telling myself that's why I feel so warm and not the heat coming from his hand in mine.

He breaks the gaze and stares down at our hands intertwined; I try to pull away, but he won't let go. "It took us a while to figure it out."

"Figure what out?"

"The different types of love. I love Angie. I do. And she loves me."

It should've been crazy weird to hear a boy confess his love for someone else while you held hands under the water but for some reason this didn't bother me. When Miles spoke of his love for Angie it was frank and quiet, like

Abuela spoke, his fingers gently moving across my hand. "She will always be a part of my family—she *is* family . . . like a sister. Not a girlfriend."

A sister. It felt like a hundred butterflies were kissing my skin. Tingles ran up my spine, my heart lightened. I did not contain them. The butterflies control the water, float me toward him; we are inches apart as his eyes find mine. I think of straightening, placing my hands on either side of him. It would make me much warmer—skin to skin. I blush at the thought.

"Does she feel the same?"

"Sort of—she thought we had just gotten into a routine, but it wasn't even that, we had become a—damn, this is hard to explain."

"You should just word vomit it." I reach over to the edge where he's sitting, pulling myself closer, and he grabs my hand, tugs, and now I stand right in front of him.

"I'm trying. I swear." Miles keeps stroking my hand, searching for the words. "It sounds so simple, but we were best friends, then boyfriend and girlfriend, and then we just went back around to best friends again. Love, but not in love. She got there too, eventually."

"You broke up?" I need to know.

"Yes."

I fight the smile. Don't smile.

"So you don't have a girlfriend?"

"No."

"Even though you said you did, just a moment ago." I gesture over my shoulder as if that is where the past is kept.

"Right. Right." He exhales. "It's been a long time since I've spoken of her as anything else. I guess now she's just Angie."

"So why did you run if she is a *had* and not a *have*?"

"Little bit of everything. I want to stay friends—I love her." Miles looks up, searching my eyes for anger but finding none.

"I don't think she believes me."

"She's scared of losing you. I would be too."

I can feel the rain running down my back, and I wonder if it is okay to hang out in a heated pool during a storm? Probably not.

"Yeah," Miles says, his touch on my hand distracting me. I should pull away so I can concentrate on what he is saying, but I selfishly stay. "Taj and Danny know, but it's not my place to tell her friends, and . . . and I just didn't want to lie and I didn't want to think about it anymore because part of me did have doubts; because I'm seventeen and what the hell do I know about love, right? What if I'm just messing it all up? It's not like there isn't other shit on my shoulders and I can't lose Angie, but she deserves better."

"So do you."

"Hmmm." His breath deepens. I watch his chest rise, droplets rolling down. He jumps back in with me, still holding my hand like it contains the answers he needs. Turning it over, he runs his fingers over my palm pausing on the crescent-shaped scar just below my thumb then up to my wrists, bringing it up to his lips, kissing it. His lips are soft, wet; my pulse beats against the touch. He pulls me forward, and I thank God we aren't talking anymore because who can form sentences at a time like this?

He wraps his arm around my waist, so perfectly warm even as the rain and bitter wind try their best to chill us to the bone. We are flush against each other, lips just a hairsbreadth away. I am mesmerized by every bit of him and wonder if I've possibly just made him up, a figment. Miles traces his lips against my cheek, dropping his head on my shoulder, taking in the feel of my skin, and I follow with mine on his. We sway a bit, the water lapping around us. The rain pricks, but it is nothing like the feel of his skin below my hands. If I could dive into him and disappear I would. I can feel Miles playing with a strand of my hair, the gesture both calming and possessive.

He tilts my mouth up, running his fingers over my lips. He traces the raindrops as they run down my face, my mouth. He brings my lips to his, encompassing. And though the rain doesn't disappear and the wind doesn't cease, they are nothing compared to his lips, his body with mine, to the heat under my hands. *You are nothing, storm. Try as you might, you are nothing.*

The melody to "My Darling Jean" plays in my head, and I hope the whole world can hear it.

LITTLE MISS

Little Miss, I,
I don't know how—I
had never seen
such a bright thing
with fairy wings. I—I
couldn't breathe.

We felt the sway,
the tug and play
of the Midsummer scene.

So it wasn't long
just a couple of songs
before we became
a couple of flickering lights
in the heat of the night
in the heat of everything.

Little Miss, I—I
don't know how, I
had never seen
such a bright thing
with fairy wings. I—I
couldn't breathe.

And even though our
history is shorter
than it's ever been.
When you take my hand, I—
I can see that our paths
were meant to cross.

So, Little Miss, I—I
ask you to stay
and help me be.
Because with you—I
have been the brightest
I've ever been.

Global Warming

THE QUARTER IS ALMOST A GHOST TOWN WHEN WE EMERGE from the hotel, from our kiss, secure in each other's warmth. The streets, which once were throbbing with people, now only bustle with the sound of rain against rooftops and the shriek of the wind as it picks up speed. It is unsettling and surreal, particularly compared to the energy that strums between us. Miles's kiss is still fresh on my lips. I press my fingers against them as if I could feel the memory there. Instead I feel the thump, thump, thump of my heartbeat— an instrument just played—and Miles thrums beside me. In my head I hear our different beats, colliding, mixing, falling into place; a song not quite there yet but soon. Soon. He watches me, eyes lingering on my mouth.

We gravitate toward each other as we walk.

"Where is everyone?"

"I have no idea." Miles reaches for my hand, and together we travel along the streets, meandering around discarded cups and remnants of costumes. The pavements glimmer as we walk—the result of sequins and glitter sacrificed to the night.

"Really hope the zombie apocalypse didn't happen while we were in the pool," I say, trying to lighten the mood, but I'm secretly searching for zombies around every corner.

"If it did, you'd have to keep me safe. I do not do well with decomposing bodies." Miles makes a face and does his best zombie impersonation. It is horrible.

"No worries, I'll protect you," I say, even though I know we would be dead within minutes if this were a true zombie event of cataclysmic proportions. I have absolutely no useful skills and would only serve as semi-good moral support. I can't even make it through a slasher film without hiding my face in Kara's shoulder.

"Can we stop over there for some water?" I motion to a pharmacy up by the road.

"You spent over an hour in a body of water, and you're thirsty?"

"Yes, chlorine makes me dehydrated."

We head on up to what's actually more of a twenty-four-hour convenience store, but when we walk in we get a bit of a shock. "You sure the apocalypse didn't happen?"

The shelves are practically barren—from the entrance I can see there's only a gallon of water left and no smaller bottles whatsoever.

"What are you two doing here so late?" A woman comes barreling toward us, carrying a large sheet of wood. She looks about sixty with bare arms that are toned and muscular.

"It's only, what?" Miles turns to me. "One, two?"

Which is late by most people's standards but perhaps not by Mid-Summer standards, plus the night feels like it just started.

She leans the sheet of wood by the cash register, then picks up the hammer and a couple of nails. "I know what goddamn time it is. I don't mean that, I mean the hurricane. Didn't you hear the news?"

"No," I say. "We've just been walking around, and no one else seemed worried about the weather as far as I could tell."

"That was then, honey, and tides change."

Miles adjusts his banjo and says, "I thought it was an offshore storm, and we were only going to get a lot of wind and rain."

Which we had. I figured the actual storm would just be more of the same but for a longer period of time.

"Like I said, that was then, this is now. It was a tropical storm and we were just going to get the ass of it, but now it's a damn Category Two and it is going to hit us straight on."

"Oh."

"Damn straight." She picks up the plank once again and walks past us. "Supposed to feel it sometime around four, five in the morning."

"We still got time then," Miles says, looking at me with a reassuring smile.

"I'm taking no chances—closing for the night and heading for my cousin's up the way. I suggest you do the same, though I don't know why I bother wasting my time. That hurricane is going to traipse its ass straight through New Orleans, and people will still be in the damn bar."

"Mind if we get some water?"

"Get what you want; you got ten minutes—gotta get home and board up my windows before I leave. Can't afford no stinkin' broken glass, and I'm getting tired of fixing stuff around here, been fixing shit for years now. If you don't mind I'm going to board up the store while you two peruse to your heart's content. Give us a shout when you're done."

"All right." Miles heads for the shelves, grabbing the last gallon of water.

"Shouldn't we head back . . ." I don't finish. *Back where?* I think. Back home, back to Tavis? Neither option is appetizing.

"Or we could stick it out, get some water, snacks, hole up." That last bit he says while looking at me through the world's most persuasive eyelashes. The boy is good.

"But the hurricane . . ."

"It's a Category Two. It's not that bad."

"Did you learn this in weather school?"

"Yes," he says with a wink. "Listen, Katrina was a five. This is nothing in comparison. If we hole up we can keep this going. Plus, weathermen are always wrong about how soon a storm is going to hit. It might be two hours from now, it might be one. Safer to hole up now just in case. I promise we'll be safe. I know a nice solid building, above ground, sturdy as hell. Withheld the last couple hurricanes after Katrina like a champ." Miles continues browsing the aisles and snags a bottle of hard cider. His eyes meet mine. "I don't want this night to end just yet."

His voice is almost pleading, and truthfully I don't want the night to end either. The thought of spending a dark candlelit night surrounded by Tavis and the cheer squad is the polar opposite of appealing, unlike a night holed up with Miles, which would be, well . . . Plus I'm not ready to face my punishment just yet. I press down on my scar, my decision becoming clearer and clearer. I mean . . . it could be JUST around the corner. Really it would be the safest choice.

"We're going to need more than just water and cider."

"Yes!"

Miles pulls me into his arms and gives a quick hug before releasing me; I wobble a bit as we turn back to the shelves.

There's not much left, so we end up with the gallon

of water, the bottle of cider, an apple, a box of crackers, gummy candies, one Twinkie, a few tiny candles, and two giant Santa Barbara candles. By the time we go up to pay, the woman will only take twenty for all of it—which Miles and I split—because she doesn't have time for change.

"You think this is that global warming shit they've been talking about for years?" she asks while she stuffs our items into bags.

"Uh . . . maybe?"

"Knew it. Been saying it for ten years, but no one listens. You got a goddamn storm destroying everything in its path, and we're still using Styrofoam cups like we don't know what's up." She's boarded up the windows and is flicking off the lights as we exit the store. "Get yourselves home!" she yells as she follows us out and clicks the lock.

"Yes, ma'am!" Miles replies, and we wave as we continue on.

There are a couple of more people out now who also seem to be buying food and water and are heading back to wherever they're going to spend the night. The lack of drunk people wandering the streets keeping the party going is a bit alarming, but Miles assures me they're somewhere in the city, probably at a bar waiting on the last minute to head home.

"What's this building we're holing up in? Are we going back to the hotel?"

"Nice guess. There's a floor they use mainly for storage

and supplies. We'll be safe there. We need to be above-ground in case there's any water damage and leaks."

"What about windows? Don't things fly around during hurricanes?"

Light shines off the pavement as we dash our way back to the hotel. Pockets of water create tiny mirrors along the sidewalks that reflect the light from the streetlamps.

"They do, and we want to stay as far away from them as possible. There's a storage closet filled with old furniture we can stay in, no windows to speak of so we should be good to go."

"Are you sure about this?" I stop in the middle of the street, the wind wrapping itself around me, pushing me against Miles. It's getting into the scary strong category and I wonder if people ever get carried up into hurricanes the way Dorothy got swept away by the tornado in *The Wizard of Oz*.

"Are you? Lila, it's okay if you don't want to do this." Rain is pooling down his face, and he's blinking like crazy. "I'll take you back home and that will be that."

He doesn't mean home, of course, home would be a two-hour flight and a lot of yelling. But he doesn't know that. Here, back would mean Tavis, who wouldn't yell. He'd reach for my hand and be sorely disappointed in me, asking me to share my thoughts with the group, to explain how I was feeling and why I believed the only option was to run. Pushing and pushing.

"No. No, I want to keep going."

Miles nods and pauses for a moment as if giving me another chance to back out. "Cool. I need to ask a favor first."

"Okay."

"I know we said no cell phones, but I need to check in with my family, make sure they're okay. I'll tell them I'm with some friends in the Quarter or something. I just need to know everything is fine."

The rain soaks into my clothes, pools in my hair, and drips down my face. "Of course. Can you check on Taj and Danny as well?"

Miles smiles, making me feel much better about my decision.

"Thank you, I will."

Fishing his phone out of his pocket, we duck underneath a balcony, the rain still more of a heavy mist. Our clothes are already so wet, what is there really to salvage, but neither of us feel like standing out in it, and who knows how long this conversation will last.

Miles's phone pings with incoming texts as soon as he turns it back on. "Your mom?"

"Yeah—and my dad too. Give me a sec." He dials his mother, and she picks up pretty quick. "Hey, Mom. Yes, I'm okay . . . phone died . . . right. Sorry, I know, I know. Yeah, Danny and Taj hooked up with Angie's friends and I didn't . . . yeah, exactly. No, I'm with Brian, from school . . . family has a house in the Quarter. Yeah, it will be safer here. Well, I suppose we owe Mr. Al a big ol' thank you for helping with that, and you know he'll never let us forget it. When are you all heading up? Okay, don't wait for me. Yes, I'll be fine. You taking Angie and her family? Okay, cool." Miles's gaze flicks over to me, a question in his eyes. "Yeah—I'll keep my phone on. I promise."

There's no way I'll force Miles to shut his phone off during the storm, he's probably just as worried about his mom as she is about him. I nod okay, and Miles goes back to the conversation. A blessing, as the panic rushes back in—my parents must be panicked, they must know about the hurricane by now and they're calling me only to have their calls go straight to voice mail—if my mailbox isn't too full to accept new messages. I have no idea what Adam must be thinking—he must know that this all started with him, but I can't bring myself to check my messages. I can't go back—not now. I should call my parents and let them know I'm all right. I should call Adam, text Em and Kara. Apologize for being so damn selfish. The high-staticky sound that accompanies the memories floods back in the second I give it some space. My breath becomes labored, and I lean against a building concentrating on the rain and on Miles, how it felt to be in his arms, his lips on mine. How I know he trusts me even though he just met me.

And I wait for the static to pass.

Give Me Shelter

I RUB THE SCAR ON MY HAND AS MILES FISHES OUT THE KEY TO the hotel from its metal box and thoughts I'd had of asking him to take me back to the youth group fade. Will my punishment be any worse if I wait for the storm to pass? Probably not, and I need more time.

Miles looks over at me. "Ready?"

No static. No pitch. Just Miles.

"Ready."

Our arms brush against each other as we enter the tiny hotel. Miles walks over to a panel on the wall and plugs in some numbers before we venture farther in.

"Alarm?"

"Yeah—I set it back on so we need to make sure we turn it off before we go opening the front door."

It's dark inside. Miles keeps his hand on my waist and makes no moves to turn on any lights but there's enough coming from the windows. Inside, the furniture is sparse and covered in white sheets; an iron chandelier sits in the middle of one room, wires hanging down from the ceiling. I dally, pulling Miles with me as I tour the variety of paintings on the walls—some appear to be big blobs of paint on canvas, others large strokes in bright colors, and some incredibly detailed recreations of New Orleans houses.

"Local artists. Most of the stuff here is," he says, head nestling into my shoulder. "Actually probably all of the stuff here is."

I lean back as I examine the brushstrokes in a painting of the Quarter houses, stalling but I don't care. Neither does Miles. We've been stuck in each other's orbit since the kiss, any separation quickly amended by the brush of a hand.

Suddenly animated, he hops into the next room, motioning for me to follow. He points out a set of clay skeleton men standing in a row on a nearby table. They are no bigger than eight inches tall, painted a matte black with contrasting white for the bones. "These are my favorite. They represent one of the New Orleans Krewes."

Each skeleton holds an instrument or object of some kind to set him apart from the others—a guitar, a saxophone, or just a top hat. I reach over to touch one, the texture rough against my skin.

"They're beautiful."

"Plus, the heads come off, I think." He gently pulls on one of the sculpture's heads, and it pops off in his hand. The rest of the body is shaped like a bottle, open at the top.

"Are they going to be okay out here? They look a bit delicate."

To prove my point they all rattle like restless spirits—or really expensive bobbleheads.

"You worry too much, Lila."

"I don't think that's always a bad thing."

The heads continue to shake, seemingly in agreement. Miles obliges, and we move the little men inside a cabinet, laying them down and covering them with cleaning cloths as if setting them to sleep.

"Better?"

I smile, and we trudge up the stairs to the top floor and down the hall. Our way is slow, and I run my fingers over the smooth wood railings and take in my surroundings; from the lacquered steps to the sculpted lace encircling each of the delicate chandeliers, everything is so carefully restored. It's hard to tell in the dark, but I have a feeling that the colors on the wall are as vibrant as the Louisiana sunset I saw today. The rain pumps up the volume, slamming against the windows; we made it just in time. The doors to the guest rooms are unlocked so of course I peek into as many as possible; each has its own color scheme taken from a piece of art in the room. We move past them down the hall.

"No fancy room for us, then?"

"You looking for a bed, Sunshine?" He advances, pressing up against me, hand at my back. Not forceful, loose, yet challenging like we're about to dance the tango. I stare him down, a playful smirk on my lips; I don't blush. Challenge accepted.

Miles winks and gives me a smile so wicked that I swat him on the shoulder. This is fun. I might actually be a natural at this flirting stuff.

The room we end up with is more of an oversize storage closet containing a few stacked boxes, an old couch probably used by the staff to take naps on, and some cleaning supplies. No windows to be seen.

"Not bad, right? We'll do just fine here," Miles says. I'm not sure if he's trying to reassure me or himself.

"Looks secure." I walk in, brushing my hand on a nearby dresser. It's covered in dust, and I clean my fingers on my jeans. "Not that I've ever been through a hurricane."

"Aside from leaving the area depending on how bad it is, the rules are basic: high ground, sturdy building, stay away from windows, stockpile the water . . . So yeah. We'll just need to figure out how to pass the time." He leans against the wall and gives me the world's most exaggerated wink.

I roll my eyes and turn away. He chuckles and pulls the supply bag from my hand, organizing our stash near the couch. He sets his banjo near the wall and starts to kick off his shoes. Miles tugs at his shirt, a flash of skin. I toss my bag near the couch, then remember the dirty construction shirt in my bag. Who cares if it stinks, just let it be dry. As soon as my hand reaches in I know it's wet, everything is. Ugh. I take out the shirt and my phone, laying them all out on the floor to dry.

My socks are wet as well so I toss off my shoes and cozy onto the couch. Miles plops down next to me, and the couch gives a pitiful groan as we settle.

"So."

"So."

I'm unsure of where to start back up again after our conversation in the pool. I want to hear more about his life, but it feels so unfair that he's offered so much and I so little, but still . . . the wet shirt sticks to his chest. *Look somewhere else,* I tell myself.

He extends his arm on the couch behind me, picking up a strand of my hair. His touch travels all the way to the base of my neck before it keeps going.

I tuck my feet underneath myself, my jeans not as stretchy when wet, and search for another benign subject to drone on about. "Well then . . ."

"Tell me more about yourself," Miles says as if reading

my mind. "Doesn't have to be anything from the deep, dark depths of your soul. I think we've done a pretty good job of skirting around those issues."

I kick him across the couch, and he holds his hands up. "Kidding. All I'm saying is that as much as I'd like to give advice on places not to be in at night in New Orleans, I'd rather hear about you. Anything about you, really, so I can remember."

I nod. I can hear the patter of the rain on the windows outside in the hall—how long would it take before that patter became a pounding?

Suddenly, Miles hops off the couch, searching through a nearby cabinet, pulling out a deck of cards. He sits down on the floor, patting the area right in front of him. "Let's make this interesting. Lose a hand, and you have to share something, anything. Wait." I freeze like I did back in the cathedral, waiting for his voice to unfreeze me. "Green light," he continues, "scratch 'anything': don't want just some random information; it must be something good, like don't be rude—this is poker—you gotta play for the high stakes."

I sit down across from him, ringing the excess water from my hair. It makes a tiny stain on the hardwood floors. Miles holds out his hand to shake mine. Another deal. I should probably tell him I'm not exactly new at playing poker. Adam taught me when I was ten, and Abuela Julia taught him. I should probably tell him that. But I don't.

Miles is so screwed.

The deck is pretty worn out and yellowed from use. I shuffle them, and they move easily between my fingers. I cut the deck, dealing. Miles tries to break up my amazing concentration by making faces at me from behind his cards. He has no idea what's coming.

The first round is a warm-up. I lose. Fine. But I lose the second one too.

Miles is a horrible winner. Horrible.

"Ha!" He throws his cards on top of mine like we were in some crazy high-stakes thriller, playing for millions. He jogs a mini victory lap around our tiny hideaway then pretends to be so winded he collapses next to me.

I shake my head, holding back my smile. I don't tell him I let him win, that often losing is the best way to figure out other people's styles. How they bluff, what their tells are. It's only been two rounds, but I can already spot Miles's tells when he has a good hand: his shoulders straighten, he holds his cards closer to his chest, he tries very hard not to smile. He is toast.

Granted, figuring this out cost me information.

"Pay up." He motions with his hands like I'm handing over a stack of bills.

"Anything?" I say.

"No." Miles shakes his head. "Something good,

remember? Like"—he shuffles the cards for the next game—"who taught you how to not play poker?"

Rude.

"My brother."

"You have a brother! Fantastic. Tell me more."

"His name is Adam."

"Strong name, very biblical."

I shake my head, a smile threatening to sneak through.

"Sorry, sorry. I'll keep quiet, I promise." He places his hand over his heart, then changes his mind. "Nah—I'm going to keep asking questions. Older or younger?"

"Older."

"Why did he teach you poker?"

"He taught me a lot of stuff, and I pestered him until he caved."

"So he's a good big brother then."

I pause for a moment, about to answer before I realize that what Miles said was a statement and not a question. Yet it still made my heart skip with its certainty—because Adam is a good big brother, he is—but for a moment, and just for a moment, I had to think before I could respond.

I settle the cards between us. "Yeah, he's good."

"No fighting and shit?"

"I don't think that makes or breaks a good big brother really."

"Just trying to get you to talk, Lila."

I nod, tugging at my shirt. It and my jeans have super-glued themselves to my body. My skin feels itchy and cold, and I wish there was a way to dry them a bit. "He's a good brother. He just got back from a tour of duty."

"Whoa. How long was he gone?"

"A year."

"Shit."

"About right."

"But he's back now?"

I reach over for the cider and take a small sip and nod, avoiding his eyes. "Yeah, he's back."

I pick up my cards, ready for a next round, when the lights flicker out and we're plunged into darkness.

"Don't move, Ace." I hear Miles shuffling for our bag of supplies and the soft clink of the Santa Barbara candles as he places them on the floor. He lights one and uses the lit candle to place the other smaller ones around the room, leaving one or two still in the bag for later.

It takes a moment for my eyes to adjust to the soft glow from the candles around us. The room looks so different now, way more intimate than it was before. Memories of the pool rush back, I let them. These are much better memories to drown in. I consider snuffing out the candles and continuing our previous activities, but a girl's gotta kick ass first.

I win the next hand. Miles shakes his head, narrows his eyes.

"I see how it is."

I shrug my shoulders. "Pay up."

"That's just mean, Lila. Would your grandmother approve of such methods?"

I laugh, reaching for the cider. "She didn't need them. She made everyone talk to her whether they liked it or not." I take another swig, smiling against the mouth of the bottle. "Everyone. Mom wasn't allowed to recap anyone's day, like she would lie or something. We each had to get on the phone ourselves so Abuela Julia could hear it straight from us, and she would get so snippy when we dallied or said 'like' too many times. I think she got everyone to spill all their secrets that way."

"You miss her?"

"Yeah." My fingers brush the surface of the cross. "I could've used her no-nonsense style this year." My voice fades as I hand the bottle over to Miles. He's watching me, and I realize he's figured out my tells as well. Sneaky, sneaky. "Don't try and change the subject. Pretty sure you lost, so my reward, please!"

"I don't like what this game has done to you." He slaps his cards on top of mine. "Aren't you tired of my story?"

"No—not at all." I pick up the cards, my turn to shuffle.

I deal. Miles gathers his cards, holding them tight to his chest. "A grandparent for a grandparent then. My gran-gran."

"Gran-gran?"

"Yes, Gran-gran and Gram-gram. I was not a very creative little kid. What do you call your grandparents?"

"Pretty much Grandma and Grandpa, but Abuela Julia was always Abuela Julia unless I wanted to be snarky, in which case it was Doña Julia, and she would follow it up with a '*Qué mona.*'"

"That's what I thought." He rearranges his cards a little too much, pairing them up. "Gran-gran likes to leave half-empty glasses of water, juice, and milk all over my aunt's house, claiming he'll clean them up eventually or that he's saving them for later. Gram-gram says he's just an old fool who can't remember where he left anything, and my aunt agrees when she's not fighting with Gram-gram over what is appropriate attire for a woman her age and in her field."

"How old is she?" I switch out one card. Miles, three.

"No idea, but she's a physics professor—and I guess she doesn't dress like one."

I win this hand and continue my line of questioning.

"Why do your grandparents live with your aunt?"

"Can't really afford a 'daycare' as my Gram-gram calls it, plus they're family." Miles pauses, clearing his throat. "And since we've had so much to rebuild, our house—his house—isn't good for them. My mom says as the youngest it's my aunt's duty to have no life and take care of them . . . but that's a point of contention." He reaches over and plucks the deck of cards from my hands and starts shuffling. "In front of me, they talk about it all joking with exaggerated gestures. But I think there's a kernel of truth to it, you know? Like when you say 'just kidding' at the end of some screwed-up statement like you didn't mean it, but you did?"

I nod. Taking care of the shuffling will not help him, but I'll keep that to myself. "Your grandfather built your house?" I motion over to the gummy candies. Miles reaches for them, and his shirt rides up, another flash of skin before a bag of gummies is flying toward my face. I just narrowly catch it.

"Not all by himself, but yeah." He deals the cards, gathering his own. His shoulders sag a bit and he grimaces. "He built things all his life—natural talent, my mom says— kind of still does, according to my aunt."

"Probably leaves his tools around the house too."

Miles laughs—this time it's a single shout followed by a small burst. I'm addicted. His laugh makes me smile, and I wonder what else I can say to make him laugh like that again.

"He does, he totally does. His stuff is pretty cool; he'll just gather all these random objects and weave them together to form a birdhouse without even thinking about it. Aunt Olivia says he's slowing down, though, his hands aren't as quick as they used to be. Pisses him off a lot."

"But he still does it?" I keep my cards, Miles changes one.

"Yeah, takes him longer and sometimes they look like

shit, but he keeps going. He made this bracelet actually."
Miles runs his fingers over the delicate chain. I reach forward without realizing it, and he lets me pull his hand toward me. Now that I'm getting a closer look, I can see where different bits of chain were joined together along with a narrow rectangular gold plate. I rub my fingers over it, feeling the engraving that reads "10.28." Miles pulls away before I can turn it to read what's written on the other side.

"Birthday?"

Miles nods.

"I can't believe he made that."

"He took broken pieces from family jewelry and welded it together. My dad helped him out too—it's a bit of a miracle those two managed to work together at the time. My parents were divorced by then, and my dad wanted to make me something before he headed out to Chi-town, so he asked my grandfather for help."

"Have you always worn it?"

He readjusts the bracelet in his hands. "Nah, a little when I was a kid, but then I got embarrassed by it; not many guys wear bracelets, you know? But then, I guess I stopped caring what other people thought."

"I like it."

He continues to fiddle with the bracelet, and the smile he gives me is warm and kind. "I'll let them know."

I rub my arms; the wet clothes do not help with the

chill. Miles hops up, leaving the room and coming back with a blanket and two towels. "Can't believe it took me this long to get these."

We use the towels to dry our hair and as much of our clothes as possible, which isn't much. I move the bottle away from us as Miles spreads the blanket over me. "You aren't cold?" I ask.

"I am but—"

I open the blanket, inviting Miles to sit by me.

"You sure?"

Nope—yes—every cell in my body is screaming, *What do you think you're doing? Don't do this to us, we are not cool enough for this.*

"Yes," I say. "You just have to promise not to try and look at my cards."

"You're whooping my ass, I cannot promise you that."

Em and Kara would be cheering me on, yelling lewd things if they saw any of this. Miles and I curl up under the blanket where it is appetizingly warm and fantastic. My mind scrambles, *What if I accidentally touch him?* Followed by, *What if I want to touch him? I actually want to touch him, reach for his hand, do it, do it, do it.* I concentrate on the cards. Two queens.

Images of Miles and I tumbling on top of each other on the couch invade my mind, multiplying one after the other. I smile without knowing, and Miles bumps me on the shoulder. I hide my cards. "What's that for?"

"Nothing."

"Come on." Miles stretches out his leg and starts tapping me on the knee. The image of him shirtless (he was shirtless in my imagining) on top of me is not fading fast enough so I blurt the first thing that pops into my brain.

"Was Angie your only girlfriend?"

"Uh." Miles chuckles and tucks the leg back under himself. "Not exactly . . . yeah, she's the only girl I've ever dated. Officially that is. There was Josephine Maguire, Joe, in sixth grade. We kissed every day for a month and then it was over."

"What happened?"

"She moved away. New York, I think. Then there was Angie, and who cared about anyone else? How about you?"

"Me?"

"No, the other person in this room." He tugs at a strand of my hair.

"I've had two boyfriends actually."

"Whoa."

I shove him hard. "Shut up, only one of them was . . ."

"Was?" Miles is reaching for my hand again; he holds it in his lap.

"Serious?" I think of my hand in his, on his lap. The warmth, the butterflies. "Worth it, I guess. No, not what I mean, I only really connected with one of them."

"What was his name?" Miles picks out two new cards. He has nothing. I keep mine.

"Luke. Lucas."

"He sounds horrible."

"No, that was Andrew actually."

His thumb traces down my hand and stops at my wrist. "I knew it—what did Andrew do?"

It's not my turn. I haven't lost—in fact I'm pretty sure he's about to—but I want to keep going. It feels good to talk to Miles, it's felt good all day, and though I'm annoyed at myself for waiting this long it feels right that I'm here with him and talking about it now.

"He was a jerk." I shift toward Miles, a movement that feels as natural now as holding my hand in his. "A real asshole to other people, nice to me and my friends but he would say the meanest things to others when I wasn't around. We dated for three months before I blew up at him, which was pretty big for me. I'm not much of a—I have trouble speaking up, but I did somehow and told him what a jerk he was."

"Did that make him see the light?"

"God no, he's still an asshole, even spread some lovely rumors about me and him, said we had sex and other stuff. . . . If it hadn't been for Emma . . ." Kick-ass amazing Emma who tackled Andrew in the hallway after school, calling him a total prick and threatening to "cut it off" if he didn't fess up to the lies. I think I pulled her off him eventually, but Kara and I definitely watched for a minute or two, impressed by how well Emma held her own.

Andrew did not apologize and remains a prick to this day. "He plays lacrosse now, so it's even worse because he's more popular."

Miles's brow furrows, his eyes narrowing. He places the cards between us. Nothing. He has nothing. I reveal mine with a flourish, and he places his hand over his heart, wounded. In a flash he reaches for my arm, running his hands up and down them. God—shivers, shivers everywhere. "I know you have an extra deck here somewhere."

"Sore loser." I tug my arm, and he tugs it back.

He keeps his hand around my wrist, his thumb doing slow circular movements. "Tell me Luke was nice, please. I don't want to believe you only go for jerks, because that does not bode well for me."

"I do not go for jerks—Andrew burned that out of me a hundred percent. Emma always brings it up, though, won't ever let me forget it. She'll point him out and go, 'I can't believe you let that catch get away.'"

"Emma is . . . ?"

"One of my best friends. Em and Kara."

You mean were best friends, don't you, Jules?

"They sound cool."

"Yeah—they are."

There's a pit settling into my stomach, which happens when I think of Emma and Kara and how I pushed them away. I think back to the texts on my phone from Em. Had my parents called her? Would she understand why

I ran away? Twice. Even though we haven't spoken in a month . . . or was it two? When did I stop answering their messages? It all feels like a blur now.

I plaster on a smile even I know it looks sad and continue. "We've been friends since preschool. Emma is insanely smart and wants to be a teacher when she grows up because she hates all the teachers at our school and thinks she can do better."

My genuine pride for my friends must be masking my fake enthusiasm because Miles leans his head closer to mine, eager for more.

In the distance, I hear the beat of the wind against the walls.

"Kara is basically the only reason I passed Chem. Though I confess I delete most of the information from my brain at the end of the week, so she kinda has to start fresh every time. I just can't wrap my head around the equations—it all looks like one elaborate, impenetrable code. And I'm pretty sure I know the world's most randomest facts because of both of them."

"Like? Give me one."

"A hippo's milk is pink."

"I know this," Miles says. "Because it's strawberry flavored?"

I roll my eyes. "That and the two types of acids the hippo secretes."

It does turn out I'm really good at remembering random

facts that have nothing to do with anything I will be tested on—it is apparently my superpower.

"Secrete is such a sexy word, don't you think?" He draws out the word "Seeecreeete."

I can't help it and start laughing. Miles has a smug little smile on his face.

"So acids aren't as cool as strawberry milk but still pretty cool."

"Hate to disappoint." It's my turn to rub my thumb along Miles's hand and concentrate on the feel of his in mine.

"Yeah, Em and Kara, they're both—" I think of my friends, of Kara's ridiculous smile and Emma rolling her eyes at whatever we are talking about. About Kara making a short person joke—she's a least five inches taller than both of us—and Em attempting to untangle my hair after a failed french braid attempt. I miss them so much, my breath catches. "Amazing, yeah, amazing. We joke that I'll become a librarian in whatever school Emma ends up teaching at so we can continue to hang out and solve crimes together."

"There'll be crime?"

"Petty mostly. And the occasional murder, of course."

"Of course."

Miles tucks an errant strand of hair behind my ear. "Is that what you want to be, a librarian?"

Miles traces my chin with his fingers, and I flash back to the pool, the kiss—then he lets his hand drop. I think of asking him to do that again, but instead I settle in closer. "That's more of a story. I—I haven't thought about what I want to be in a long time. I wanted to be an archaeologist when I was little, I think that's one of the three standards, right? Archaeologist, vet, and then that person in movies that just somehow knows everything for no particular reason."

Miles is shaking his head. "Not sure what you're basing your three standard dreams on, but I wanted to be an astronaut, a supercool guitar player, and a professional praline eater."

I pick up the cards again, shuffle and start dealing. My cards are horrible, and I switch out two. Meh. Just a bit better.

"Why archaeologist?"

"Archaeology is about finding people's stories and preserving them. Sounded pretty cool. Still does actually."

The wobbling tower of books in my room is a testament to that. I have so many books on myths, legends, history, folktales, anything I could find. Notebooks filled with stories I pried from Abuela Julia before bed, my friends at school, and, when I annoyed her enough, Em's mom. Miles touches my cheek, bringing me back to the present.

"Was Luke nice?"

"Yes. Luke was very nice. Is still very nice, actually."

"He's the serious one, right?"

"We dated for a year and a half."

Miles whistles. "That's long. Why did you break up?"

Unlike my relationship with Emma and Kara, the dissolution of Luke and I had nothing to do with Adam. We'd broken up before he'd gotten back.

"He liked someone else."

"He cheated on you?"

"No, no. He met a girl at a party and they just kept talking and he started getting these feelings for her and didn't want to hurt me so we broke up."

Miles nods, thinking it over. "Were you heartbroken?"

"Devastated. Emma, Kara, and I spent days just talking shit about him and all that, then slowly he mattered less. We're sort of friends now. Sort of."

"Sort of?" His brow arches, a look I immediately like.

"His new girlfriend doesn't really like that we talk."

"Why not? He's with her now."

"Reasons."

"Come on, Sunshine." He tugs at the bottom of my shirt. "Give me one secret. One."

One secret coming up—but you aren't going to like it. Time to use my mood-destroying talents.

"We were each other's firsts."

"Oh . . . yeah. I get that." He scratches the back of his neck, looking very amused at my answer. "I don't know if I'd want my boyfriend hanging around the first person who actually meant something to him."

"How do you know I actually meant something to him?"

"Because he seems like a smart guy."

My cheeks feel warm, and I think of reaching for the cider again despite that I don't really like the taste, so instead I crack open the water and take a drink.

Miles leans back on his elbows, the blanket falls behind us, his eyes still watching me. "You still have feelings for him?"

"Yeah. I mean, I don't think I loved him." It feels cruel to say, because I did care about Luke very much, but I don't think I ever loved him, nor him me. "But I really trusted him, and he trusted me. So I remember the good stuff and what made me like him and want him to be happy."

"That is incredibly mature of you."

"That is Kara talking actually—I think she should be a therapist or a psychologist, but she's determined to save the world as a doctor, which she will, obvs."

Miles nods and looks down at our stash. "What should we dive into next? I'm feeling a bit low on the sugar, how about you?"

I can still feel the sugar from the cider coursing through me, but I nod anyway.

"A bit."

He reaches over for the Twinkie. "Let's break this little one open."

The treat is equal parts stale and sweet, and we drink it down with more water. We tuck ourselves back under the blanket, the space between us disappearing once again. It feels so natural to curl into him. My body shivers when he rubs my arm to warm me up. He drops his cards, and we give up the pretense of playing another round.

"Tired of getting your ass kicked?" With my leg I hit Miles. He catches it before I tuck it back under me and his hand stays on my calf for a moment before we both shoot up at the sound of broken glass. It's followed by more glass breaking and something hitting the ground; Miles bolts off the couch.

"Stay here," he says as he rushes out. I can hear the wind, far better than I could before; it feels like it's all around us now. Above me, something hits the roof before it's dragged away. The lights flicker on and then off once more.

When Miles comes back I am sufficiently startled.

"What happened?"

"Something got caught up in the wind and flew right through a bedroom window, made a mess." His eyes flit around the room until he finds something in the back, tucked into a corner. He picks up a Santa Barbara candle and moves to the back, illuminating another section of the room, which is much bigger than I thought. I hear Miles moving boxes around, and when he comes back he's carrying a large sheet of wood in one hand, like the kind the shop owner had. He passes me the candle. "I need to close up that window before anything else comes through."

"Right." I nod, my mind already listing all the things that can travel through an open window from branches to animals to vampires to snakes. ANYTHING really.

"Lila?"

I'm still racing through all the ridiculousness as now is the time for such things when I look up at Miles.

"Yeah?"

He motions to the hall. "Will you help me?"

Pump Up the Volume

I CAN HEAR THE WIND SCREECHING THROUGH THE HALL. THE door is right at the end of our hallway, and the closer we get to the bedroom the louder it gets. Once we push open the door, we feel the wind flow in through the broken window like water in a sinking ship. As we're about to enter, I look down and put a hand out to stop Miles—pieces of broken glass lay scattered across the floor, probably aided by the wind. Miles and I quickly go back for our shoes before entering again. Though I avoid stepping on the larger bits, it feels quite defiant to hear the crunch of glass below my feet, knowing that it can't hurt me.

We settle the sheet of wood against the window, using the weight of our bodies to keep it in place, but the wind refuses to be held back. Miles holds the sheet in place as I move around the edges with my hammer and nail it down, securing it for God knows how long. This feels like just the tip of what this hurricane can do, and it's only a matter of time before these nails will no longer hold—or another window breaks.

When we release the wood, it bows and bends with each gust of wind. "Um. That's not going to last." I imagine this is why you are supposed to place these on the outside of the window and not the inside, but there's no use now.

"No, it's not."

Around the room lamps have fallen on their sides and items such as bowls and vases have rolled onto the floor. It feels wrong to leave the room like this, so Miles and I move what's left of the breakable stuff (that hasn't already broken) into the small adjacent bathroom and sweep the glass into a corner before closing the door.

Out in the hall my eyes drift down to the other rooms, and I remember the pieces of art hanging in each one. Miles looks over at me and says, "You're going to make me go into every room and hide things, aren't you?"

"Things could break! Lamps could fall! Societies might crumble!" I realize how silly I must sound and match Miles's smile with my own. "Um, other stuff can happen."

"You seem freaked out a bit."

"Well, it is my first hurricane, and I think it'll help if I keep myself busy." The wind screeches and I jump. "Once I spring-cleaned our entire garage during finals."

"See? You could be busy telling me your life story." He places his hand on my waist. "There are so many secrets to be learned."

"I thought no baggage?"

"Yeah, I know." He pulls me closer, his other hand cupping my face. I can barely hold his gaze when he leans in, the kiss so light on my lips, a brushing of skin against skin. "But I kind of want it all now."

My heart pounds. There is so much to tell—how could anyone want all of it? But I am drowning, drowning in want and the way Miles takes me in, because it's true, he would take the good, the bad, everything. I close the gap.

The wind slams up against the hall windows as if annoyed that we've ignored it for this long. We break apart, reluctant. The wind is a petulant child. I want to go back into our windowless room and hide under the covers and let every single window break when something slams against the glass and it cracks. I give in.

"You know, the faster we do this . . ."

Miles laughs and nods. "Sounds like a plan."

We head out into each room, pulling down the pieces of art and gathering them in corners or tucking them inside the giant Narnia-like wardrobes in each of the rooms. Miles makes a show of feeling at the back of each wardrobe for any hidden doors or compartments before popping back out. In one room I help him lift this gorgeous painting of a woman sitting in a courtyard staring out at some point beyond the canvas.

"Thank you for obliging me."

Miles shrugs it off. "You're right. Plus the less we have to clean up later, the better."

"We?"

He sets a lamp down beside the bed, reaching under the table to unplug it. "You aren't leaving me here to put all this stuff back by myself."

With one room finished we head over to the next. The theme of this one seems to be Regency-era chic, with the main focal point being a large four-poster bed draped in both lace and gossamer.

On the opposite side of the bed, I struggle with one particular painting as I pull it down. "My dad would like this one. He's always wanted to paint." The frame is more than four feet in length and feels like it weighs at least sixty pounds. I lean it against my thighs as Miles comes up behind me, lifting one side as I take the other.

"What does he do?"

"People's taxes." I smile, thinking of my dad. "He's possibly the quietest man alive," but maybe that award goes to Adam now. "I'm not sure he knows what to do with us anymore."

It is the first bit of deep-down truth that's slipped through, and I try to pretend there's nothing more to it.

He takes the painting from me and lays it on the bed.

"We should finish up stashing the art and head back into the other room before any more windows break."

"You think more will break?" I hop on the bed, next to the painting.

"Windows break all the time during storms, so we just want to stay away from them until it's over. And I'm not saying it to scare you."

"Right. I guess I wasn't prepared for this part of our adventure."

"That's New Orleans for ya. But a promise is a promise, Lila." Miles comes up to me, pulls me into a hug as I slide off the bed and our lips almost meet, and he shifts away with such a wicked grin. "Nothing bad is going to happen to you."

He maneuvers away from my hand as I try and smack him on the shoulder. Devious little devil. I stick out my tongue and focus on the painting.

The painting itself is kind of boring—a field and some trees, which are pretty, but a little paint-by-numbers compared to the others we've encountered. Miles watches my face, barks out a quick laugh.

"It's the frame," he says, fingers running down the wood. "Salvaged wood from one of the destroyed houses. Amazing, isn't it? You can feel New Orleans in the carving."

I take a step back toward the bed, really looking at the frame. It's dusted in gold and the wood beneath the accents is deep and rich, carved with a series of ridges that mimic the flow of water. I trail my fingers down the deepest groove until my hand meets Miles's. I stop, and his fingers travel up my arm, continuing the pattern of the frame on my skin, to my shoulder, then my neck. He shifts behind me, one hand still on my neck, the other now at my waist and sliding around to my stomach. I lean back as he does and my shirt pulls up just enough for our skin to touch. I want him to keep going and want his hand to stay where it is at the same time.

I keep my hands to my sides as we press up against the bed, pushing the painting farther down the mattress. Miles dips his head toward me, lightly kissing my shoulder, my neck, the tip of my ear; one hand trails down my back, the other slips under my shirt. My pulse picks up, and I wait and wait for his hands to continue but they don't move and it takes me a moment to realize that he's waiting for me— Miles wants me to guide him, to tell him what I want.

What do I want? I feel my hand slip on top of Miles's and guide it up. I can feel my heart thudding against his hand and each kiss across my neck and shoulder is driving me insane. *What do you want, Jules?* The thought keeps barging in as I lean farther into him and it is infuriating. I know what I want, stupid brain. I want this, I want Miles and me on this damn bed and I want to push everything, everything else in my life away so far that it will never hurt again.

I turn, pulling Miles's mouth toward me, capturing his lower lip first before I deepen the kiss. His hands travel quickly, grabbing me by my legs, wrapping them around his waist, slamming me against the wall. His lips travel down my chin, down my neck and chest. His hand pauses at the top of my jeans—a silent query—and he brings his face back up to mine.

"Maybe we should slow down a bit." His voice is scratchy, and I can barely hear it over the pressure of the wind beating against the glass.

I bring my lips back down to his as he sets me on my feet, hands traveling to my face. He shoves his hands in my hair and dips his head to my neck, staying there for a moment. The whole world seems to mute as we stand— before it comes crashing back to remind us.

In one quick movement something slams up against a window in the room, cracking the glass as Miles shifts in front of me.

"Let's go." Miles snags my hand as we rush out of the room and back down the hall and into our refuge.

"Sunshine," he says as he kisses me again, tongue lightly touching my lips. He tastes salty and sweet, and I press myself up against him, needing to be closer, as close as possible. We fall on the couch, my hands work faster than my mind and reach down to tug his shirt off. Then it's lips, hands, legs wrapping around one another, Miles now on top, pulling up my shirt and pausing at the top of my jeans. He looks up. "Yes?"

I lift up from the couch, plant a quick kiss on his lips, and smile. "Yes."

Miles flushes up against me, burying his face in my neck. His hands travel to the back of my bra. I'm shocked by how close I want to be, how much more skin I want to touch. My hands fumble at his jeans, a flash of silver from his pocket. I watch his face, a hint of red on his cheeks and just a bit sheepish as I pull them down before all hesitation vanishes.

We are rhythm. We are sound and touch and need. And it is good.

ON MY WAY

Good morning—then
go on, greet the sun,
the day already too long.

I dust myself off
And head down the way,
A groove in the floor
tells me I never strayed.

And I'm on, I'm on, I'm on my way.
Down the same path,
from which I've never strayed.
These chords feel so drawn,
and these lyrics are staid.
What is the point anyway?

Then right in my path, right in my way
this bright thing, so blazing
the sun shies away.
She lights up the paths
that I've ignored to this day.
Paths that I thought I had hidden away.

And I'm on, I'm on, I'm on my way.
This new path more vibrant
than I've ever played.

Eye of the Storm

WARMTH ENVELOPES ME. IT SLIDES DOWN MY BACK TO MY WAIST, pulling me up from my dream. The world is soft and out of focus. As my mind begins to sharpen I pinpoint the source of the heat: Miles's body pressed against mine. We are curved into each other, his arm wrapped around me, one leg between mine, a blanket halfway down our bodies.

I have no idea what time it is, and I can't reach for a phone to check. One or two of the smaller candles have started to dim, while the Santa Barbara is as bright as before. I watch the flame of the candle flicker across Miles's skin, and I let my fingers trail the shadows across his back. He shifts for a moment, arms tightening around me.

Santa Barbara is supposed to give you strength and courage during difficult times. I wonder now if I chose the candle or she chose me. I watch her flame and think that being here with Miles, I haven't felt this safe in such a long time.

I hate to stir and wake him, but my body demands it; as secure as I am, my muscles ache with a need to stretch and move. I have no idea how long we've been asleep, but it feels like hours. Lifting his arms I slip off the couch and reach for my underwear. The slight pressure in my back springs to life, wanting attention, so I stretch reaching up to the ceiling, feeling everything loosen.

"A lovely sight to wake up to." His voice is soft and groggy.

I exhale with a laugh, meeting his smiling eyes with my own. Following my lead Miles stretches, the blanket coming perilously close to falling even farther down his waist. My cheeks redden, my mind ripe with memories. I reach over for my shirt and put it on; Miles places his hand behind my knee, tugging me toward him as he sits up.

"What are you doing?"

I smirk. "Writing a sonnet."

"Really?" He caresses the back of my knee. "What about?"

"About . . ." My mind slogs through, trying to find playful answers but I come up empty. "Pass?"

His smile is a thousand watts, my heart flutters once again, his eyes lock on mine.

"Why get dressed?"

"Because."

"My favorite answer! Because?"

"Well we—"

He tugs at my knee. "Already . . . you know." His eyebrows wag in mock seduction.

"No." Words can't tumble out of my mouth fast enough. "That's not—"

"It is," he starts, that wicked grin back on his face. "Just because we're naked doesn't mean we have to have sex. And frankly, I'm surprised at how dirty your mind is." His hand drifts up my leg. "Though I one hundred percent support it."

I kick him in the shin, and he slips his hands farther up in retaliation, causing goose bumps to bloom on my thighs.

"You can stay naked if you like"—a quick kiss and I pick up my jeans—"I'm getting dressed."

"Sounds good." Miles stands, letting the blanket fall off his hips before walking over to our supplies and eating half our gummy bears. I spend the next five minutes admiring Miles's absolutely gorgeous body and trying not to stare.

After a stifled giggle, Miles struts over with the bag of gummies, offering me the rest. I shake my head, and he comes around, kissing my neck.

"What are you thinking?" he asks.

He pops several gummies in his mouth, sparking memories of his lips on mine. I twist to face him, channeling all the vintage ladies made of moxie, gumption, and silky-smooth voices that drip confidence. "Eyes up, young lady."

I run my finger down his chest; my heartbeat is out of control, but not on the outside. Outside I'm sexy and in command.

"You have permission to look all you want. I'm all yours." He takes a deep breath as I pull him closer.

"Are you?" I close the gap, my lips so close to his they almost touch.

"I am tonight." I expect another grin or cocky lift of an eyebrow but Miles is still, his face an open book. "May I kiss you?"

I nod, not trusting my words. He tastes like sugar, the warmth of him enveloping me. My hands wrap around his waist, pressing him closer as his weave through my hair, resisting the urge to give his ass a squeeze.

It's then I notice the bracelet on my wrist—it catches the glow from the candles. I run my finger down the links. "Why?"

His finger traces the bracelet and runs up my arm. "I don't"—his eyes find mine, he leans in for a soft kiss—"I don't want you to forget me."

As if that could be possible. The bracelet feels cool against my wrist. We kiss again, and when we break I explore his neck with my lips.

I'm somewhere along his collarbone when he says, "Do you hear that?"

Which is a trick question because I can't hear anything above my own pulse. "Hmm. What?"

"Nothing—there's nothing to hear."

So it is a trick question.

In a flash, Miles is out of my embrace and racing down the hallway—naked. Before I have time to register the loss, he's back with the same bounce of energy. *Oh God, eyes up!*

"It's the eye!"

"The what?"

"Put on your shoes." He's throwing on his clothes. "It's the eye of the hurricane—we're going outside."

The what now?

We dress quickly, and Miles rushes me out the door.

"Come on," he says, pulling me by the hand. "I want to show you something. It's not far."

"Isn't it dangerous to be walking around right now?" Still I slip my shoes on, following him.

I chance a look at the sky—expecting to see it wiped clean, sun shining through, but it isn't. The sky is muted, a dull gray made up of one eternal cloud. The sight of it wakes me up, reminding me we are still very much in a storm. I take in my surroundings. The buildings, the vibrant colors now subdued: a wash of gray around all New Orleans.

"We'll be back before it starts back up," he says as he ties an errant shoelace. "We'll be able to tell, I promise. The wind and rain will pick back up like angry devils. Trust me, we'll know."

He offers me his hand, and we race through the streets, debris everywhere. We zig through shattered glass, plants that have traveled great distances. The night air feels amazing now that our clothes are dry.

The damage to the buildings looks superficial so far: cracked glass, plants pulled up by their roots . . . until we pass a particular building with a broken balcony that won't survive the second half of the storm; it creaks as we make our way past.

"I wonder how the rest of the city faired."

Miles pauses to look with me. "Probably worse. The Quarter usually doesn't get hit as hard by water surges since it's above water level."

"Do you live in . . . ?"

We pick our way through the tougher debris. "I live around Carrollton, actually, not far from where you and a couple hundred people danced down the streets. Damage will be around the same; usually it's the Lower Ninth that gets the worst."

"Did your house suffer a lot of damage after . . . ?"

"Yeah." Miles's grip tightens for a moment. "Not all from Katrina—hard to keep rebuilding when shit keeps knocking you down."

"I—" I stop myself, caught between wanting to know and not wanting to ask.

"You can ask. I didn't really go into it." He doesn't turn when he speaks, guiding me again, slowly this time, a much more difficult path now than it was before. "It was enough to eat into our savings. Enough to get a loan from the bank we can't pay off."

"They're taking your house, aren't they?"

I pull Miles to a stop and he faces me, dropping my hand to lace his own at the back of his neck. He's quiet for what feels like forever, and I hope I haven't screwed things up.

His scream catches me off guard—it turns from sound into an actual word: "FUUUUUUCK."

He stares up at the sky. The gray stares back. "Yeah. They're taking my grandfather's house, that he fucking built, that we rebuilt. That my mom put her life into so that we could have a damn home and history." Anger mixes with sadness. "Just in time too, there's barely anything left to fix. They'll have a nice new house to sell if this damn storm doesn't tear it all apart again."

"I'm sorry."

He turns, a quick kiss on the lips, his thumb caressing my cheek.

"Let's keep going; eyes don't last long."

WE REACH THE river, and Miles walks ahead of me toward a wooden dock that looks like it hasn't been used since 1910. I pause before stepping on it; the water around us is beyond choppy, attacking the pier as he continues on.

"Feel like taking a dip in the Mississippi?"

I have a fear of it washing us both away as the wind kicks up. Miles does not share my worry; he pauses, turning to extend his hand. I quickly catch up. The wood creaks but doesn't budge.

"I think I'll pass." The water does not look inviting. It is brown and murky and the bit that splashes up from the shore feels cold as ice. "Who knows what the hurricane dumped in there."

"True." Miles leans back, watching the waves across the way. "This is one of my favorite places to go when I need to think. My father and I used to sit here all the time when I was a kid. Just throwing rocks out into the deep, talking about why the sky is blue, why boats float." He laughs—quietly, to himself. "I was an annoying kid."

"Still are." I wink.

"When he left it took me a while before I could come here on my own, but I needed it. I needed to just sit by the river until things made enough sense or it was time to go home." Miles reaches over, grabbing a few pebbles from where the wind has scattered them along the dock, and tosses them in one by one. "I wanted you to see it. We didn't get to see all of my New Orleans, but at least there's this."

"Does it work? The staring."

"Give it a try," he says, shrugging.

I look out into this body of water—it stretches far beyond my vision, waves still raging across its surface, a reminder of what came through and what's still to come. I can feel Miles next to me, watching. He's a surprise I wasn't expecting in my life. I close my eyes, the sound of the waves against the shore burrowing deep into me, pulling things out of me with each receding wave. I feel the hollowness that I've tried to avoid for so long come simmering to the surface, freed by something, either the water or Miles or time, but something opens, something is ready and I spill.

"I—I walked out into traffic," I start, already feeling lighter, as if I'd been holding my breath all this time. "That's why I'm here in New Orleans."

Miles places his hand on my back.

"I didn't realize," I say, but it's not true.

I knew I was doing it. I knew. I heard the horn and I snapped out of my daze just in time. I hated myself for doing it and another small part of me hated myself for not going through with it.

"That's a lie." My body starts shaking, rebelling against my lies. "I knew . . . I knew what I was doing. It wasn't, it wasn't thought out or anything, I just, it all became too much, and I thought that if . . . if I'm gone then all of that goes away." I wrap my arms around myself. "I didn't think it through, I didn't think past the promise of it all being gone." I meet Miles's eyes, unsure of what to expect. The kindness I find in them almost pulls another sob from me. "I'm not even making sense, am I?"

"You don't owe me sense. You don't owe me anything, Lila." His arms envelop me. Together we are warmth and light and hope. I rest my head on his shoulder. If I break, will he able to hold me together? "I'm just going to listen."

It is several breaths before I can start again. I speak about Adam. About my awesome big brother who always protected me, about him leaving and coming back different and wrong. Knowing that I needed to help him and how I'd failed. I failed him and he'd failed me. "I thought I could help, that I could magically turn him back into my brother. That all he needed was us. Didn't he see we were there?" I grip his shirt, which feels soft beneath my fingertips. I open my hand and press it against his chest, tracking his heart-beat. "When he didn't . . . he kept rejecting me and I was so angry because I was a failure and we weren't enough, enough for him to try, and that made me so angry. And then I felt guilty, then angry again. Then I couldn't hold it in anymore. He wasn't going to try—I could see it. He was just going to keep drowning."

The water splashes up the dock.

I flash back to that day, to the screaming, trying to calm both Adam and myself down. How Adam's face didn't look like his own. My hand on Miles's chest balls into a fist at the memory.

I feel Miles's hand on my cheek, grounding me. "My parents drove around looking for him, but it was no use. We waited. My dad fell asleep on the couch. In the morn-ing, there were two cops at our door." His hand stills. "Adam was alive. Sleeping it off in jail. The girl he hit—"

Annalise. His shirt soaks up my tears. "She was paralyzed. Is paralyzed."

I let out a breath. "I keep going back, to the door, to the cops, to the thought that popped in my head."

"What thought?" He strokes my hair.

"I thought, he's dead." I close my eyes, picturing the two officers at my door, my breath catching. "Then I thought, it's over. It's all over, he got what he wanted. Release. It was just a second—a moment of relief that his pain was gone before the guilt and shame roared back in." I take a deep breath.

"When I go home the police want me to testify against my brother. About the problems, about that night. They want to build a case against him since Annalise's parents haven't pressed charges. I don't know what to do. People look at me like I did it. I look at me like I did it."

Miles's arm tightens around my shoulder.

As my mind fights back through the gray and fog, there isn't much left, but what is left feels clearer, not lighter, but valid, and that validation feels good.

Miles doesn't say anything; his hand is gently rubbing my back as I lean into him. The words come before I'm sure they're ready. "Everything is messed up, isn't it?"

"Doesn't mean it's not going to get better," he says.

"I'm not sure I'm there yet."

Miles pulls me up to face him. "What about this? You and me. Tonight. Damn, Sunshine, it's already better for me." His hand caresses my face. "Do you have any idea?"

◆

"Of?"

His voice is a whisper. "How bright you shine."

I shake my head. Such a pretty thought, but I am not bright, not as far as I can feel it.

"Don't you shake your head." He pulls my face up, the kiss so deep it hurts to stop. "I know what I see. A light so bright everything else disappears. And I'm not looking for a second opinion."

"We still have to go back. Home, I mean."

His hand pushes the thought away. "That's later. Later can go screw itself. Now is pretty stellar."

My hand rests on his cheek, I remind myself he is real and he is here. "Stellar, huh?"

"Yeah. Damn stellar. Everything about it. You."

I rub my face, wiping away the tears. "I need you to look away because I need to blow my nose and I'm going to use my shirt."

He laughs but turns. "You do you."

My body is still shaken from crying. I hiccup and blow my nose as quietly as possible and thankfully there's not a huge glob of snot at the end of my shirt, though I wipe that part on the ground next to me just to be sure. I rub at my eyes, warning any future tears that they too shall be dealt with. And Miles waits beside me, shielding me from the gusts of wind that are getting stronger. His hand in mine keeps me tethered to the now. It stops me from slipping back to the past.

He draws me in, kissing me. It is less urgent this time, gentle, but no less deep and encompassing. We take our time until we feel the wind circle around us, another set of hands closing in. His lips travel to my cheek. "Time to head back."

For a moment, anxiety creeps in before I realize that our time together is still not at an end.

"I like the way you think," Miles says.

My eyes narrow, head tilts. "How do you know what I'm thinking?"

"I'm hoping we're thinking the same thing. And I'm pretty sure we are."

I pull him in, bold, unhindered by bashfulness, for another kiss. One hand wraps around his waist, the other settles on his neck, and his phone buzzes against his hip. I pull away, releasing a loud fake groan as he checks his cell.

"My mom."

"Of course," I say, keeping my voice light.

"Mood killer?"

I shake my head. His brow lifts.

"Two minutes?"

The wind whips my hair up, and pieces of paper and debris slap across my legs.

"Two minutes."

Miles picks up his phone. "Everything okay?" he starts. "Yeah—no damage over here yet. Lost electricity though."

I drift back toward the water, still agitated, waves now

growing in strength. I mentally run through the route we took to get here and how fast we'll need to move to avoid getting caught in the tail end of the hurricane. It should be no more than five minutes. Water splashes on my face from the waves that crash against the pier, and I am hypnotized by the way they fight against this structure in their way. I want to be off this pier before the river wins. I can hear Miles wrapping it up with his mom as my eyes cut out to the river and down the shoreline.

"Mom? MOM?"

I turn. "What's wrong?"

"The phone cut off."

"Maybe her battery died?"

"It's a landline—my aunt is old school." He's fidgeting, dialing the numbers again and again.

"Did she sound okay?"

"Yeah, yeah. I'm just—"

I move toward Miles when the wind pushes me back with a shocking strength. Toto, we are definitely not in Kansas anymore. I regain my balance, shaking off the thought that the air and wind are alive and need me out of their way enough to lift me up and carry me away.

"You okay?" Miles's hand is in mine in an instant.

"I think we need to leave."

"Right. Right." He takes one final look at his phone before he puts it away.

"I know you're worried. We'll keep calling her at the

hotel, okay? Once we're safe behind windowless walls."

"Let's go." He nods.

A piece of flying newspaper slaps against my leg, then another. I pick it off and the wind snags it from my fingers, a violent tug and the paper snags and rips as it is carried away. As we make our way off the dock, tiny pebbles prick our skin. *Pain,* I think, *like Abuela Julia mentioned.* You know you're in trouble when the wind becomes painful.

When the wind is alive.

We make it off the pier. I should feel safer now, on solid ground, but something is off. Something feels wrong and I can't place it but I drag my feet waiting for my mind to catch up. I feel ludicrous. *Pick up your feet and go, Julie!*

"What's wrong?" Miles asks.

I shake my head. "I—I don't know."

I reach for the now familiar feel of the metal against my wrist. Finally it clicks. It's gone.

Miles's bracelet is gone.

Good Intentions

REALLY IT WAS ALL MY FAULT THAT EMMA AND I WEREN'T TALK-
ing anymore—100 percent. Though tell that to my
emotions. As far as their logic is concerned, Emma was just
as much to blame as I was. But, really, they can't see what a
giant bag of crap I was being to my best friend. And Kara?
Well, I guess that's on me too.

And, really, I've been the one giving them the silent
treatment like a ten-year-old. There hasn't been a moment
when Emma and Kara stopped texting, calling, emailing,
dropping by to see how I was doing. I'm the jerk in this, if
there was any doubt in anyone's mind.

Days after Adam pinned me to the ground in his sleep,
he still wouldn't meet my eye. The nightmares continued,

but I no longer knocked, no longer pushed open the door to see how he was doing; my hand remained permanently hovering over the knob, paralyzed by something I couldn't figure out. I still can't. Was I afraid for Adam or afraid of him? That question, even now, can't encompass all the complicated thoughts and feelings rolling around in my mind. As far as I was concerned there was a door and I was on one side ready to knock. But there was also the memory of the pressure on my neck and a weary walk back to my own room. The echo of rejection.

Emma and Kara pried the truth out of me as only friends can. We were in the park, hanging out on the picnic tables, killing time. I had zoned out for the third time during a conversation about the many things that could kill you in Australia (short answer: everything) and why we should cross it off the list of places to visit when we were rich and famous, when my hand traveled to my neck again, rubbing the skin.

"Stop doing that." Kara leaned over to pull my hand away. "Your skin is all red and blotchy. Did you fall or something?"

"Are you okay?" Emma asked.

"Fine." I smiled and waved them off, eager to get back to our usual top-ten- (now twenty-five) places-we-want-to-visit-before-we-die discussion. "What other venomous snakes live in Australia?"

"A quicker question would be what venomous snakes

don't live in Australia," Emma said. "Also, don't 'fine' us. We don't get fine. Fine is for your parents, Facebook friends, and ex-boyfriends. No fine."

"Seriously, I'm—"

Em shook her head, not having any of it. "Nope. Kara?"

"You've been off."

"Off?"

Kara nodded. "Off. And to be honest, I'm—*we* are not sure why. I feel like we haven't talked—like, *talked* talked—in forever."

"I know I'm cuing the cliché dialogue here, but you can tell us anything." Emma smiled as Kara reached over interlacing my hand with hers. "And if you don't, you know we'll just start jumping to conclusions—which we're really good at."

"Amazing at," Kara agreed.

"Practically a superpower," Emma continued. "Right now I'm jumping to unrequited love, a horrible robotic experiment gone wrong, and something to do with a lost dog."

"Or all three!" Kara interjected, giving my hand a quick squeeze for dramatic effect.

"All three!" Emma shouted. "See? We're on a one-way train to Conclusionville and we need to be stopped."

I managed an actual real-life smile. "That makes no sense."

"Exactly. So . . . ?"

Emma leaned toward me, Kara squeezed my hand again—these girls, my girls, how could I not trust them? Yet it was so hard to get the words out. I felt myself retreat again, tumbling down into a void and not fighting it whatsoever.

"It's Adam."

I looked up—thinking for a moment that the words had tumbled out of my mouth, but no, it was Emma. Her dark-brown eyes bore into mine and I realized I'd been avoiding her all day for this particular reason. It was impossible to not cave to Emma's stare. A Liu family trait passed through from generations of women; Emma had it in spades.

I spilled everything on that picnic table, emotions, thoughts, tears, not caring what they understood and what they didn't. Kara rubbed my back, which turned out to be a facilitator for more secret spilling. They listened, they asked if I was okay, they asked for more details. What else was happening? What else had Adam done? Did I tell my parents? Why not?

Their questions kept repeating in my mind, a sick echo of fault and guilt. I regretted opening my mouth and felt I'd somehow betrayed Adam by telling Kara and Em about what had happened, so I shut down and they backed off. The bell rang, and we went our separate ways.

Later that night, Em texted me, begging to meet again for a chat at the park the next day; she and Kara came prepared, which wasn't surprising; they were super researchers. They must have spent hours looking things up online and probably regretted not having days to work on securing secondary sources and expert testimony.

"So," Kara started, exchanging glances with Em. She sat right next to me while Emma sat across the table. "Emma and I were talking about Adam and the attack last night."

"It wasn't an attack," I bit back. "He didn't know what he was doing."

"Okay, okay." Emma nodded. "It wasn't an attack, but we looked some stuff up on the internet, starting with medical sites, then went into our little black holes of research. You know how we are."

Oh I knew; if you searched long enough you could disprove every thought in the universe.

"And we found some information that could be useful. Kara?"

Kara's smile was meant to be reassuring, but it was too late, the walls were built. "So we started by, like, looking up nightmares and violent—um—incidents in veterans and kept coming back to post-traumatic stress disorder."

Disorder. The word echoed.

"There doesn't seem to be a consensus on, like, how much time you had to serve to get it or actions related to it."

"Actions? Like nightmares?"

Emma jumped in. "Meaning if it's connected to the stuff they did during the war or something."

"Yeah—that," Kara said.

I shook my head. "I don't know what he did; he won't

talk about it." This was a lie, I never once outright asked Adam about the things he did in the war. Perhaps in a way I thought I *was* asking every time I said, "Are you okay?"

"What else did you find?"

"Well." Emma pulled out a pile of papers, highlighted in sections and filled with tiny, handwritten margin notes. "I printed out all the articles I could find with medical references—there's a lot. Different symptoms depending on the person, of course, but there are common ones."

"Like?" My heart sped up, my hands shook.

She shuffled through the mass of papers. "Disinterest in life and daily activity. The nightmares—with some morning episodes, I think—trouble reintegrating into their lives before military service. Most of it is what you would expect, I feel like, of someone coming back from service. There's this one particular article that I found interesting—it's all about PTSD and how it's related to morality and guilt." Emma paused, hesitant to continue. Kara picked up where she left off.

"There are also incidents of violence too."

"He didn't mean to hurt me," I jumped in. I pulled out Abuela Julia's cross, tugging it down until the metal dug into my neck. "You should've seen his face, he was so lost when he woke up." I closed my eyes, pushing back the memory of the broken look on Adam's face.

Kara settled closer on the bench, her hand reached for mine, unhooking it from the chain. "We don't think Adam meant to hurt you, we swear. We just think he needs help."

"Like professional help," Emma clarified before I even thought of suggesting that I could help Adam just fine. They knew me too well. "I spoke to my mom about it."

"Whoa, you what?"

Holy shit, this is not happening. How could she?

"Em, it wasn't your secret to tell! I haven't even told my parents—"

"I didn't tell her it was about Adam." Her hands reach for me, trying to calm me down. "I just asked her, like, a hypothetical situation."

"Oh yeah, hypothetical situation? Did you mention the army stuff?"

Em didn't look at me; her hand stopped halfway down the table.

"You shouldn't have said anything. Of course your mom is going to figure it out!"

Next to me Kara jumped in, "Stop yelling at her; she was just trying to help."

I picked up my bag, shoving the stack of papers inside. "We're done."

I stormed off, Em and Kara calling after me, begging me to sit and talk. I didn't stop.

AT HOME I took the papers out, dropping them on my bed, unsure of what to do. Should I give them to Adam? Should I give them to my parents? How do I know that

Adam has PTSD? What if—what if I screw everything up by suggesting that he does? Maybe he's just having a hard time adjusting and here I am talking about disorders and seeing doctors.

I glanced through the pages and pages of symptoms, history, where to find help, but my eyes focused on one particular article: "The Incidence of Suicide Among Those Suffering from PTSD." I rushed through the article, picking up percentages here and there. My heart was racing and I had to stop at one point to stick my head out the window and get air. I felt like ripping the pages in half, but instead I dropped them in a drawer and slammed it shut. The fear that Adam could take his own life now infected every space of my brain, overloading it. My room felt too small. I started to shake, and I couldn't hear my heartbeat, it was going so fast. I ran downstairs, building the walls of the dam that would be the beginning of keeping these thoughts at bay.

I could hear my mom in the kitchen. The smell of store-bought cookie dough, a smell that usually makes me happy, now making me sick. In the kitchen my mom was rinsing out her mug and filling the kettle with water before placing it on the stove. I went straight to her and wrapped my arms around her.

"This is nice." She leaned back against me. "What's the catch?"

I couldn't respond. I was still pulling myself together,

brick by brick. My stomach settling.

"Julia?"

"I don't know what to do."

"With what?" She rubbed my arm.

"Adam."

My mom stilled, releasing a heavy sigh as she pulled my arms from around her belly and turned to face me, her brown eyes taking a good look, just like Abuela Julia used to do. I held on to the ache of missing my abuela, secure in its familiarity.

"You're worried about your brother."

"Yes."

"*¿Por qué?*"

As if on cue my neck twitched and my hand went to scratch at my skin but instead picked up the necklace. "I think he needs help."

The kettle sounded; she dropped a bag in, poured, and set the cup down to steep.

"What makes you say that?"

I looked up at my mom, her warm brown eyes that now smiled readily and held no hint of a sadness that was there before Adam returned.

She waited, patient as always, ready to listen when I was ready to speak. My abuela would not have been patient. She would have demanded to know what I was trying to say; she would have make me stand there until whatever burdened me was laid out on the table. *Why aren't you here? I need you here.*

"Just let it go, *niña*," she'd say. "What is the point of holding in such things? They fester inside and rot you from the inside." And they do. They root down to my core, a pit of ache in my heart growing and spreading through my veins.

"I'm just worried."

"You said that. Is there a particular reason?"

"Just"—I shrugged—"in general. I mean, I don't really know what active military service is or what it means to come back from it but I think, maybe if he had someone to talk to, he would feel better."

My mother nodded, sipped at her tea, and carried it over to the table. "You think your brother needs someone to talk to?"

I took another sip of mine, forcing the hot liquid down my throat, using the pain to move forward. "I think everyone needs someone to talk to. Don't you?"

"True." She reached over for my hand, and I placed mine in hers. "And it sounds like a good idea, *amor*. I'll talk to your father about it, and we'll look into it."

"*¿De veras?*"

"Of course."

Of course! How could I have been so silly? After all the fear, the crying, feeling like I was utterly useless, it was done.

Of course my parents will fix this, I thought. Of course they could see that Adam needed help.

This was the moment.

The change in the tide that shifts everything.

The point in time we would look back on and mark and remember. From here on, everything was different. From here on nothing was the same.

So simple I should've done it earlier.

Washed Away

I AM NOT HALLUCINATING. MY WRIST IS BARE. AROUND ME, THE wind picks up every piece of scrap whirling it like a blender. Sound is a banshee, hunting and beating on us; alive, screeching in our ears as the rain chills us to the core. This is why hurricanes have names—they are alive, beasts of anger, power and force. Gods reshaping the world as they please.

"You okay?" Miles tugs at my hand, and I keep looking back at the space where his bracelet used to be.

"It's gone."

"What?" He inches closer, unable to hear me over the sound.

"It's gone!" I point to my wrist. "Your bracelet. I just had it."

There's a flash of sadness in his eyes before he shakes his head. "It's okay, it doesn't matter."

"It's not okay."

Miles trusted me with it. His grandfather friggin' made it. It was full of his memories and now our own, and I let it slip away from my wrist.

I reach to my own necklace, imagining the loss I would feel if it disappeared. "Please."

Miles seems to understand that I'm not going to move until we at least try to find it.

"One minute," Miles says, knowing we might have less than that. We both drop our heads, searching the area around us. I panic; the wind is grabbing every little leaf, cup, and torn newspaper that isn't nailed down and twisting it up to the sky—what if it took the bracelet with it?

Miles spots it first, a glint in the middle of the pier, just a few feet from us.

"There." Miles drops to his knees and pulls the delicate chain out from between the planks, fixing it back on his wrist.

"Time to go," he reminds me.

I nod and he moves to rejoin me. One step and his foot breaks through the wood, caught on a rotten plank. I move toward him, but he holds up his hand to keep me at bay. He tugs his leg up, ripping his jean. The pier creaks, a death gurgle, whatever resistance it had against the storm gone.

It gives, shattering into the rage of the Mississippi and swallowing Miles whole.

This isn't happening. Miles was standing in front of me and now he's gone. I hurtle myself to what's left of the pier, not caring that it could take me with it. All I see is darkness, muddy water, hundreds of ripples across the surface.

No, no, no, no.

I want to scream and shout but I am silent, searching for something, anything. This is my fault. I should've kept going. I should've sucked up the blame and guilt over the bracelet and gotten us back to the hotel.

I shake off the voices, concentrating on the water. Where are you, Miles?

Then a flash of color. Miles's shirt.

It's all I need to dive in after him.

I don't think—just wish to be stronger, faster. The water wrenches him away from me—dangling him like a prize out of my reach. I wish I was a better swimmer—I'd hoped I was a better swimmer.

I want to scream for Miles, but the water invades my mouth before the words can come out. I carry dirt into my belly with every stroke. The water rushes in my ears, covering up the yowl of the wind before it bleeds back in at full force. I can still feel the ground below my feet but I can only balance for a second before I'm carried farther out.

Then Miles is next to me, and I can reach out and touch

him and he is real. The Mississippi is playing with us, but I won't bite.

We try holding on to each other as we swing toward the shore, but we can't. We knock against each other, slowing down. We have to let go.

"Sunshine," I hear him say, a brush of a hand.

"No," I reply. "Keep swimming."

We inch forward. Progress. Before we were slogging. My foot touches the ground underneath and relief comes like a flood, before a wave drags me under. I sputter, continue paddling. I hear Miles calling my name somewhere. The sound is too far away, and I'm too afraid to turn my eyes away from the shore.

"Almost there," I tell myself, Miles, the river. "Almost there."

And I am.

I can just barely stand. Miles is to my right; he shouts my name to let me know where he is. The river carries branches with it; they hit me as I go. I push them away; they can't slow me down. I will drudge myself through the mud and twigs and every stupid thing you throw at me.

"We can do this," Miles shouts from a few feet ahead of me. "We can do this."

I feel stones beneath my shoes, and I use them to move forward.

But the river is not ready. It sneaks around me, branches

tangling in my shoe like hands pulling me under. Will the damn world stop kicking? *Just let us get to shore, just this one thing and you can keep beating me up, I promise.*

"I'm caught—keep going," I say. When I don't see Miles move, "Go!" I yell again—no time to waste on waiting. We aren't far from the shore and the water is now at my waist. I reach down—blind—feeling for the tangling thing. The rain pounds against the river, against my face, howling, a declaration of power.

I look up. Miles has turned back and is coming for me.

"It's okay," I say, finding the branch that has its hold. "I'm almost free." My hands are clumsy and the water is not. It thrashes me down, each wave hitting its target, chipping at what little strength I have left. It wants to rip me from the tangle and take me away.

The fighting is so hard. My eyes shut and I think of sleep, of drifting off and just letting go. I'm back on that sidewalk, taking that corner, walking into the street.

"Sunshine!" Miles is the horn, blasting me back to the present. I keep fighting.

Another wave pulls me down.

The river tosses me around like paper in the wind, amused, ready to teach me how little I mean to it and the universe: a speck in the current, easily carried away. I slip under the water, bringing my hands forward, then back. Move, move, move. When I come back up, I am no closer to safety but Miles is closer to me. I focus on him.

The water hits my face. *Why do you even try, little girl?*

Please, my muscles say, *please.*

"Please," I say back. I feel the necklace along my neck, the water whisking it back and forth. It holds. *"Sigue, sigue."*

The current pulls me under, my eyes open, the world out of focus, muddy, fading. I think I see Miles swimming toward me. I shouldn't be able to. I blink and he's gone, and she's there. Abuela Julia. She reaches for me, and our hands meet.

My lungs burn. I swim toward her, and she fades.

Enough. I yank the branch up and out of the riverbed. When my shoe still won't budge I pull it off and then the other in case it has any ideas of getting caught as well. I can't see Miles anymore, just sheets and sheets of rain. If I wasn't scared I would marvel at the patterns the water makes as it slams down into the river.

"I'm late," I hear to my left. Miles is back at my side.

You turned back, you idiot, I try to say, but only "Idiot" comes out.

A grin; he spits out water, gripping my hand so tight his nails cut through my skin. The river rips through us, wrenching us farther from the shore. Where is the shore? Oh God, where is the shore?

Stow the panic. There is still some ground below my

feet, and I use it to push myself toward where I think the shore is.

Miles falls first, dragged away from me by the current until I pull him up. The pattern of the rain shifts, a moment of clarity, and I can see our destination. The shore is so close, so close. And the more I say it, the more it is so. Because that is how life works, isn't it?

Out of the corner of my eye, I see a long dark shape under the surface of the water, it's too big to be moving as fast as it is. The word "crocodile" flashes in my mind, and I am suddenly so angry.

But it's too misshaped to be a crocodile. Either way it's coming toward us, but my mind doesn't understand how close it is, that it's in our path. The river is all around us. It fights us, we push through, we continue to pay no mind to this shadow, we don't move from its path. I will keep—I will keep against the water.

But it is not water, and when it slams into me it takes what little strength I have left, except for Miles. His hand is still around my wrist, keeping me anchored. He would hold me there forever if he could. But the river has other plans. It slips between our fingers, inching them apart, it pushes into me, insistent.

There are much better things down the way, chéri, we promise.

The river's promise feels like a melody. The kind my body, beaten and tired, needs right now.

The water reaches down my throat and pulls out memories, dangling them before me. When I was eight we visited Puerto Rico with my grandmother. I met far too many family members I could never keep track of. We went to the beach, filled with families just like ours. My parents lazed by the palm trees, and I don't remember where my grandmother or brother had gone. I skipped off into the water, on my own, a little confident fool swimming out by myself. The waves took me down to the bottom and dragged me for a ways before I even thought to fight them. When I broke the surface, I was farther out than I'd ever been. I was too tired to make it back. But I did, somehow I did. Not all the way, but far enough where they would see me, far enough to matter.

Come on now, the river says. *Come on.*

I am slipping out of Miles's grip, but I hold. With my other hand, I push away what I can now see is the splintered body of a tree and give it over to the current, certain I am free, when the ground disappears below me. My grip slips, but Miles does not, his hand remains. I am screaming and coughing and screaming, my wrist in agony, ready to pop from its socket.

"Don't stop kicking!" I hear Miles yell. I find his eyes, and I can see how scared he is. And then my hand is out of his and I am battling the river on my own. The water, carrying earth and so much more with it, comes toward me. I dive under to avoid the debris and push through. I will make it, and when I win I will be in another state perhaps, but I'll make it.

The rain slaps me across the face.

Jerk.

I go down again. I push back up. I keep going. I hear Miles yelling, but I can't place how far he is from me. I am smacked around by half of New Orleans's trash, which floats with me in the Mississippi. I feel my skin open, water pouring in. It burns and I use the pain to live.

My feet find solid ground again until something slams against me and pulls me up. It's Miles. "I'm sorry, I was trying to get to you."

I search for his hand and find it. Together we battle the current, feet finding earth, one foot in front of the other. We pull each other up whenever the river decides to play with us. The water is at my waist now, and I can see the shore, the gathering of rocks that will welcome us back.

We are there; we are there.

Then I am under. Miles's hand tight around me, slamming me into the water and away from the shore. I turn to him, the wave swallowing him, a gash on his forehead pouring blood.

"Miles!" I scream, but he's not moving. I try and pull him closer to the shore with me, but he's heavy and the water is trying to carry him away. "Wake up, wake up."

Both hands on him now, dragging him out of its clutches, praying my hands won't slip, wishing I could get a better hold. If I could just wrap my arms around his waist, but I can't risk getting caught in the current, ever waiting to snag him back. I feel my way back to the shore until I hit the rocks, almost dropping him.

We are there, but we aren't safe. Everything presses against us—the wind, the rain, the debris, pounding, pounding, pounding—and I drag myself and Miles onto the shore.

I collapse on the rocks, Miles at my side, unmoving but breathing. My vision blurs, the darkness creeps in, but it doesn't scare me.

I am good. I fought. I am free.

A Crescent-Shaped Scar

WHEN THE GLASS HIT THE GROUND IT SHATTERED MY CONCEN-tration; the stanzas I was trying to remember for AP English shocked right out of me.

My parents weren't home—they'd left to visit a friend of my mom's for the day. It was a few days after my mom and I had our talk about Adam and nothing had come of it yet, but it felt like everything was going to be okay. Like it was just a matter of time.

I ran down the steps, the smell hitting me first. The closer I got to the kitchen, the stronger it was. Adam was cursing as he threw a hand towel over the spreading amber liquid on the floor. When he saw me he held up his hand. "Don't come in here—it's already a mess."

"Need help?"

"No." He threw two more towels down and moved them around with his foot. "I'm fine. It just fell; that's all."

"What was it?"

"Whiskey."

The smell—I would recognize it now, but then I was still pretty new to the different kinds of alcohol and my repertoire only extended as far as beer and tequila.

"Dad's whiskey?"

"Yes." He was irritated, shoulders bunched, picking up the larger pieces of the bottle and tossing them in the sink. "Dad's whiskey, all right?"

Adam dumped the soaked towels in the sink and shook out the smaller pieces of glass. "I'm fine, Jules, just go."

I stayed, wetting a paper towel and moving in to help. As I bent down to gather the smaller pieces of glass, Adam grabbed my hand. "I can do this, Jules." He was so fast that I slipped a bit, planting my hand to balance myself, and a glass shard sunk into my skin. I wrenched my hand away from Adam. The blood was slow to gather and the shard was only halfway in, but man did it hurt.

I felt Adam hovering behind me. "I'm sorry," he whispered, his voice taking me back to when we were younger and he'd broken something of mine or teased me until I cried. "Julie. I'm sorry."

"I was just trying to help."

"Yeah, I know. I . . ." He was gripping the towel in his hand like he was going to rip it to shreds. Then, just like that, all the tension was gone, his shoulders slumped and he extended his hand. "Let me see."

I hesitated. I didn't want to but I did. When I put my hand in his it felt like a test, but I wasn't sure who was taking it. Adam was gentle then, guiding me toward the kitchen counter, placing my hand over the sink. "It's not that bad."

Drops of blood ran down the drain. "Still hurts."

"I believe you." The corners of his mouth lifted.

Adam retrieved the first aid kit Mom kept in the kitchen.

"I don't think we'll need stitches," he said in a mocking tone, but his eyes were worried.

He ran water over the wound. I tried very hard not to wince when the cold hit my hand, but I jumped anyway. In one swift movement, Adam pulled the glass out with the tweezers and it felt worse than it had going in. Blood flowed down my arm, and Adam pressed down on the cut with a piece of paper towel before cleaning it with the alcohol and putting a Band-Aid on it. Within a minute the Band-Aid was soaked, and we changed it for a new one.

"I need stitches."

"You need stiches," Adam echoed. He threw the shard into the sink so hard I jumped again.

"Don't worry, it will stop eventually. It's not that deep." The cut was deep, but I didn't want to cause a fuss. I watched the blood pool below the second Band-Aid, and I pressed down to slow its flow. I could feel Adam's eyes on me. He grabbed a paper towel, folded it, and placed pressure over the cut.

I noticed the small tremor in his right hand. "Why don't you let me help? We can finish faster and replace the whiskey before Dad figures out it broke." *It broke—not you dropped it.* "We can put the towels in the washing machine and mop the floors. It will be like nothing happened."

Adam checked the paper towel on my hand, the blood was already slowing. "Okay," he said, and we set about erasing the last couple of minutes. Once the kitchen was scrubbed, we dropped the whiskey-soaked towels in the washing machine and headed out. Adam looked more animated than I'd seen him in a long time—like he was getting a second chance to redo this morning. And me, I was on his side, making it happen, partner in crime.

At the strip mall I stayed in the car watching as he went in and came back out with a new bottle and something else. I didn't catch what it was before he shoved it beneath his seat and started up the car. I picked at my cut for the rest of the trip, gauging how much pain I could take before I flinched.

"Checking to see if it still hurts?"

The bleeding stopped but the cut was open, gaping, and raw below the paper towel. "Yes."

"And?"

"It does."

Adam kept his eyes on the road. "Good to know."

"Think it will scar?" *Like yours,* I thought. *Tell me how you got those scars.* The voice inside my head was so clear and strong, nothing like the one I used to speak out loud. *Tell me the whole story,* it said.

"Probably."

I ignored the voice and lightened my tone. "Think it will make me look badass?"

The side of his mouth twitched. "Sure, kid."

From beneath his seat came the sound of glass meeting glass.

"What's in the bag?"

"Whiskey."

"And . . ."

"Whiskey."

I nodded. "In case you drop another bottle?"

"Yeah." He paused, hands tightening around the steering wheel. "Sure, kid."

Something clicked. I was staring out the window, watching the thin strips of white on the road fade below the wheels, the trees blur, all to the soundtrack of the *clink, clink, clink* of those damn bottles.

I hadn't wanted to see it. I thought the smell was from the broken bottle, hadn't I? Had I really? *Clink.* And what, he'd just dropped it accidentally? *Clink.* And how much liquid did I actually see on the ground?

Clink.

And what about that tremor?

I reached back under his seat, and the bottles smacked against each other as I placed them on my lap. I took a bottle out, feeling the weight of it.

"What, do you want some?"

I pulled the other bottle out. "How much did you have before it fell?"

Adam didn't answer.

I pressed down on my cut, feeling the rush of pain that overpowered the fear. "How much?" I asked again.

He let out a breath, quick. "Just let it go, kid. I'm fine."

The bottles clinked in my lap, mocking me, their joyful sound triumphant. I hated them.

"You aren't fine," I said. I opened the window and dropped both bottles out, watching them crash into the road. The sight of amber liquid staining black delighted me.

Adam slammed on the brakes—we were lucky there wasn't anyone behind us and that we were wearing seat belts.

"What the fuck, Julie?"

"What the fuck, Adam?" I replied, taking off my seat belt and rubbing my neck. Adam was out of the car and opening my door in seconds, pulling me by the arm.

"What the hell is wrong with you? Do you have any idea how much that cost?" He pointed at the smashed bottles a few yards down the road. "I thought we were in this together!"

I nodded, not in agreement, but to settle the thoughts

in my head. The sight of the broken glass, the sound of his rage, spurred me forward. I decided to let everything go before doubt or fear caught up to snag the words from my mouth. "That would require both of us to actually try, Adam."

He turned away from me, building his own walls taller, thicker, stronger than mine.

I needed to attack those walls, and I needed to do it now. "Why won't you try, Adam?"

"You think I'm not trying?" His voice was thick and coated in anger and shame.

"I don't. I think you're falling and you're not picking yourself up. I think you're shutting us out."

I waited for a reply but one didn't come.

"I want my brother back, jerk. I want the motormouth who used to talk all the time about the stupidest crap, so much stuff I didn't care about, just to torture me."

A ghost of a smile.

I kept going, encouraged. "Like that one time you talked to me for thirty minutes about how they discovered Velcro, just out of the blue, with no segue into the conversation at all. I miss that. Or the way you used to pretend you didn't like it when Abuela beat you at poker." Deep breaths. "Where are you, Adam? Where did you go, and why do you refuse to come back? It can't be that nice of a place. Not if you have to drown in whiskey."

He rolls his eyes. "I don't drown in whiskey."

"You swim in it." My hands started to shake. "I'm afraid of you, Adam. And I'm afraid for you. I think you need help, and I asked Mom and Dad to find you help and—"

He rounded on me. "You did what?"

My voice was losing its ferocity. "I told them you need help."

"Are you deaf? I don't need help, Julie."

"You do." Tears streamed down my face as I continued. "You do and they see it, even though they're afraid of losing you."

"I'm fine; they aren't going to lose me. You aren't going to lose me. You're being a child."

I stomped my foot on the ground just like I used to when I was younger. "You aren't fine. And that's okay, you just did a tour—God, Adam that HAS to have done something, and I think you have PTSD."

Adam laughed and that was worse than a foot stomp or tears. He'd dismissed me. "Don't, don't talk like you know what that is."

The street was still dead silent. I prayed for a car to drive by, to cut the tension.

"I looked it up on the internet and—"

Adam's smile was cruel, a face I didn't recognize. "Oh, amazing. Please tell me everything you've learned from the internet."

"Emma and Kara—"

"Do not tell me you brought your friends into this, Jules."

There was something to his voice, a callousness, that sent shivers up my spine. This was not going the way I'd hoped. Adam should've wanted help, he should've wanted to get better. Things were supposed to get better. Instead he pushed his fists against the hood of the car until the metal gave.

"You tried to choke me." The words were out of my mouth before I knew I'd said them.

"I—" Whatever he meant to say died.

"Come back, Adam." I steadied my voice and wiped the tears from my eyes. "I miss you, and I know, I know I won't get you back, not a hundred percent, but I'm afraid that if I don't fight for you now, that if you don't fight, I won't get any of you back." I walked toward Adam to meet him halfway. "Please let us help you."

"I am back," he said, straightening up, pulling the keys out of his pocket. "This is all that's left."

He got in the car and took off, leaving me on the side of the road.

I probably made that damn cut worse than it was. I pressed my thumb into it until it throbbed. I peeled off the scabs and scratched until it was raw, over and over again. I needed it to still be fresh, to still hurt, because then I hadn't wasted time. I hadn't let Adam down. I still had time to help.

My dad tried to track him in his car but never found him. My mom and I called all his friends, begged them to let us know if Adam had stopped by, but nobody had seen him. I wandered around the neighborhood searching for his car, praying that he had just driven down the block and parked someplace nearby while he cooled off.

It was not the first time I prayed to Abuela Julia for my brother's safety, but it was the first time I felt guilty for doing so.

HERE'S TO REMEMBERING

Here's to forgetting
your smile and your grace.
The way that you blush
when I look at your face.

Here's to forgetting
the night that we had
the secrets we shared
our souls laid bare.

Here's to forgetting
impossible things.
The feel of my heart
and your wicked grin.

Here's to remembering
the taste of your lips
the feel of your hips.

Here's to remembering
feeling alive
missing you the moments
you're not by my side.

Out of the Darkness

WHAT HAPPENS TO YOUR BODY WHEN YOU FALL ASLEEP? IT IS still there—in bed—of course, resting, but what is that? You close your eyes and time continues and you just lay there. How strange is that? The time is gone and you wake as tired as when you first felt it pull you down. And that's what it is now—a blink—I remember the river, fighting, my body giving all it had and my mind shutting down, a light dimming, my eyes closing and it is gone.

"You see that nice young man? . . . So many injuries today . . ." The voice is like a song. So very different from the siren screech of the hurricane, which is gone. Gloriously gone.

My mind reaches up from the darkness toward the voice.

"You think you'll get lucky?"

A second voice, deeper.

"Hope so." Her voice drops. "Need . . . sweet smile to brighten my day."

Music, no—a laugh. "You are too old!"

"Young at heart, honey."

The voices fade, but I keep pulling at the space they occupied. Making my way up and out, pushing through the fog to Miles. *Miles.*

I flex my hand, feeling fabric underneath my fingertips when I should be feeling his skin. Where is Miles?

My eyes finally open to a light so bright it slices through me. I lift my hand and something comes with it—wires, ropes, what is this? I search an encyclopedia of words in my head and all I find is "dangly hospital things." That can't be right.

"Don't try and pull that out, honey," I hear as someone enters the room, a different voice from before. My vision is still fuzzy around the edges, and it takes a moment for the woman to come into view. Her braids are gathered on her head like a crown, with a few strands falling across her face. "Can't spare IVs on anyone today. Need all we got."

IVs equal dangly hospital things. I nod. My head is heavy, every part of me feels like one giant pulse. How is it possible to feel this much?

"Everything"—I lick my lips, my voice cracking, dry— "feels broken."

"Mm-hmm." The woman picks up a chart from the foot of my bed and jots something down from the monitors. She smiles at me, and it is tired but sweet. "Let's see, we got a sprained wrist, about a dozen cuts and scrapes, and a bruised rib. Not to mention the minor concussion, but we've been monitoring you all day, so you're in the clear for that one. You're a lucky girl."

"Lucky?"

"Got a couple of people weren't that lucky. . . . Storms always hit us harder than we think." In the bed next to mine, a woman leans hunched over holding another woman's battered hand. My feet peek out from under the blankets; a few of my toes are a dark-purple color, and when I try to move them there's a sharp pain that makes me wonder if she forgot "broken toe" in the list of injuries.

The nurse places the chart back on my bed.

I sit, a sharp intake of breath as every part of me shoots with pain. I can feel the batch of stitches along my arm. Another tighter section along my shoulder.

"Want me to wake Romeo up?" He points toward the right of my bed, near the windows, to a slumped figure. For a moment I think it's Miles—my heart leaps, then stumbles as I gather all the details: no beautiful blue hair or dark skin, no long legs that can't be hidden. It's not Miles. Tavis is crumpled to my right, arm in a sling, head resting against the wall.

"Been here for a couple of hours now." She offers me

another sweet smile before she turns.

"Was there anyone else?"

"Far as I know, but haven't been on shift for long. I can ask one of the other nurses if you want?" I'm too slow to answer, and she places the chart back on the foot of my bed. "If you need anything there's a button on the side of your bed."

The nurse is gone before I can ask her for the other nurse or any nurse who can tell me about Miles. But she's down the hall and I'm left alone with Tavis for the first time since I ditched the prayer circle a lifetime ago. An empty sinking feeling seizes me that something terrible has happened to Miles. I think back: How far away had I gotten? There'd been solid ground below me, I know there was. Tavis shifts, I hold my breath. *Just don't move*, I tell my body. He settles again.

How quietly can I get out of bed before he wakes up? I test the needle in my arm—am I ballsy enough to pull it out? Tavis stirs. No! Go back to sleep. Or, you know, just go back.

"Hey there, Jules." Tavis rubs at his eyes, stretching before reaching for my hand.

Please don't touch me. Please go away. Please leave. My body is angry. I don't want him here, not anywhere near me. This is not who I need.

"Julie," I say instead. "My name is Julie."

Tavis ignores the comment, touching my leg. I inch

away, and he drops his hand. "How are you feeling?"

"Do you know where he is?"

"Where's who?"

"Miles." I say—then remember that's not his name, it's the name I gave him. "Where is he?" My voice wavers a bit. I close my eyes, concentrating on the pain.

"Hey. Hey." Tavis sits down, I want to jump out, but I'm not sure how far I will get. "Everything is going to be okay. We found each other, that's all that matters. You're safe now."

I shake my head, willing my mind to remember something, anything that will tell me where Miles is. I go back to the river, his hand slipping out of mine, his voice screaming for me.

"He's tall, has hazel eyes and blue hair and . . ."

"Who was tall?"

"Miles," I say again. *You aren't listening to me.*

"Jules, you aren't—"

I'm reaching for the call button. This exchange needs to end.

"Julie. My name is Julie. I need to speak to the nurse, I need to know he's okay. He was with me at the river." The rest is gibberish. I begin to sob because Miles is not here, because Miles was in the river and I don't know if he made it out.

Tavis rubs my back. I cringe and roll away. He reaches for my hand, trying to take the call button and calm me down, but it does the opposite. I swat his hand away and press the button. I press it again. No nurse.

"You and I are lucky to be alive; don't you understand that, Julie?"

I understand—I more than understand. I understand that Miles might be dead. That no one was there for him, took care of him, kept him safe. He was all alone. I pull at my hair, curl into myself, angry at Tavis for opening his stupid mouth and then angry at myself for thinking that Miles is dead, for surviving without him. And that is the clearest thought. It feels like pressing down on my cut. It sears through me and brings me back to the present. Miles is not dead. He is not dead until I search every spot—no matter how long it takes.

I don't want to be lost anymore.

I rub my face with the hospital blanket, gathering my thoughts. *What is the quickest way to get rid of Tavis?* Each time I look up he's waiting, waiting for me to want something from him. To want him.

"I need food—I'm starving." I turn to Tavis with what I hope is a convincing smile. "Can you get me something?"

"Don't think the cafeteria is open . . ."

"Vending machines?" I try again, reaching over to touch his hand. "Please, my stomach is gnawing away."

He squeezes my hand, his eyes bright. "All right, of course, you'll be okay without me?"

I pull my hand away. "I'll survive."

Tavis heads off, and I do my best impression of a healthy person and slowly rise from the bed. I feel my body booting up. I follow the cables that end in sticky patches on my chest and pull those off first—no alarms sound. I keep checking the door for Tavis. I hope the vending machines are far away, tucked in a corner no one can find or somewhere on a different floor blocked by a maze of hospital employees. I'll need every second I can get. I leave the IV for last; my hand shakes as I reach for it.

"Hey now, girl, what do you think you're doing?" A voice comes through from the past, each syllable a melody. My body sags in relief. "You trying to get ol' Julius fired?"

My eyes start to water as a familiar face comes up to me, sitting me back down.

"Like the caesar," I reply.

"Damn straight," he says. "And this here is my empire for the last twenty-five years. So where do you think you are going?"

"I need to find someone." I try to stand, and he sets me back down once again.

"You need to rest."

I shake my head—Julius must understand, it's why he's here, I know it is. He's supposed to help me find Miles. "Please, please, I don't know if he's alive, I have to know if he's alive."

He tucks my hair behind my ear, a paternal gesture. "You aren't the first person to say that to me today, darling."

"Doesn't make it any less."

"I suppose." Julius turns, reaching for my chart. "Julia Marie Eagan Hostos."

Only my grandmother and mom called me Julia. I've been Julie to everyone else since I could talk. I can hear Abuela now: *We named you Julia, not Julie,* asi que *that's what I'll call you.*

"That is a long name, darling."

"Just Julie."

"Well, Just Julie, you are a lucky girl. Lots of bumps, bruises, ten stitches."

"Just ten?" Feels like a hundred.

"Could've been worse, but you should really stay another day. Not to mention you're a minor."

"And my parents aren't here," I finish. "Did you call them?"

"Me personally? No. But I imagine someone did."

Then they'll be here soon, and I'll never find Miles—they'll never let me out of their sight after this.

"I just need to know if he was as lucky as I was."

Julius looks through my chart one more time, placing it back on the end of the bed. "You're going to pull that out the second I leave, aren't you?"

"Smart and handsome."

"Laying on the sweet talk, I see." He sighs. "What's this boy's name?"

"Well—"

Julius goes out to the nurses' station to see if any seventeen-year-old boy was checked in around the same time as I was.

When he comes back he shakes his head. I think of collapsing, of crying again, but I don't. I gather whatever strength that storm didn't take and call it forth.

Without another word Julius turns to the cabinet at the back of the room and pulls a plastic bag that looks like it's filled with mud, but turns out to be my clothes and wallet. He pulls the tape from around the IV, then gently removes the needle—I barely feel it amid all the background pain.

"You're going to need shoes."

Meet the press

Annalise Baker has a curtain of long black hair that reaches just halfway down her waist. Plaited and pinned up in a ponytail, it complemented her demeanor, her smile, and her ready answers during class. We weren't friends and we never hung out, but on occasion we shared the same exasperated look when a teacher droned on for too long. I didn't know what she wanted to be when she graduated or which colleges she planned to apply to. I knew Annalise existed and that she was happy as far as what she chose to show the world.

This is the space that she inhabited in my life and I in hers.

That is, of course, until.

The first time I snuck into the hospital, Annalise's mom screamed at me. How she knew who I was or what I was doing there I didn't know. My face had yet to make it on to the local news. I slipped in through the side entrance, kept my head down, and lurked in corners like a weirdo. I hovered, not knowing what I planned to do, or what I was expecting, what I needed to see. But my legs kept taking me there day after day.

She came like a Fury ready to peel off skin and rip into my entrails in retaliation for any wrongdoing.

And I let her.

After, I stood there feeling my skin prick as the pain—the burning—rose to the surface. I felt lighter, spent, and unsure why.

At home my phone buzzed as I entered the kitchen—another message from Em. Why won't you talk to me?

I ignored it.

My mother hovered by the sink, moving plates from sink to pantry and back again. Rearranging, cleaning, throwing out questionable preserves in the fridge. "Where did you go?"

"Walk. Where's Adam?"

Her eyes met mine only briefly before she went back to cleaning. "In his room."

I went up the stairs and right past Adam's room. He hadn't spoken to me since we paid his bail. Just as well; I have no idea what to say to him anyway. Every time I was near him our fight echoed in my mind.

In my room, I poured over the newspapers and let every sentence, every word sink in. I found Annalise's blog and fell down a black hole of old posts. I read her ramblings, her thoughts, pored over her photographs, made a mental list.

Annalise loves pistachio ice cream. Her favorite movies are all the collective works of Wes Anderson, despite the fact that she found the one about aquatic life to be not "in her wheelhouse." She got her first camera when she was twelve, and she wants to be a professional photographer even though it would be a challenging career to have. She plans on getting a second job to support this dream.

Annalise was—is—a very good photographer. Dozens of her photographs, provided by friends and family, were published all over the local newspapers. Her favorite subjects were old women with kind faces. There was a series of fifteen of them on her blog. I memorized them and recognize two of them from my own church. I imagined them posing for her while they told her their life story. I imagined she was the type of person you would tell your whole life to. Annalise liked to laugh, she hated skirts, thought aardvarks were funny, didn't like people who chose paper cups over waffle cones, and didn't really read a lot but reread her favorite novels over and over again. She had one serious relationship that she referred to with quotation marks: *"James" texted me today.*

I read and reread her entries until the words blurred. I opened Facebook and searched her name, but she didn't have a page. A page dedicated to her recovery had already sprung up with new well wishes coming in every day. I wondered how many who posted on it actually knew her.

I scrolled down until I'd read all the posts calling Adam a drunk who should've died in the accident, speculating if he was always this way or "Did, like, the war over in that country, whatever it's called, cause this?"

Not that it matters because someone totally saw him holding a beer one time or remembered how much he liked shots and doesn't that just prove that he's a drunk? I almost reply but then clicked over to my own page. Seventy-eight unanswered messages and countless posts asking me if I knew Adam had a problem, had I even tried to stop him? "I hope you get hit by a car too!" After each post Emma and Kara had come to my defense. Not that it mattered. As Kara would say, you can't argue with stupid.

A chat came through as I was closing the window. I'd forgotten to turn off the feature when I logged in.

Jules?

Kara. It felt wrong not to write her back—I missed her. I missed Em. They are parts of me that are gone and it was all my fault.

Jules, talk to me. Pretty, pretty, please?

I stared at the screen as Kara kept typing, I felt so lost, incapable of anything but drifting into my own hatred.

Kara Lee Arnold is typing.

Okay. You probably left . . . probably. Or you're
looking at this and ignoring it like my texts, which
is fine . . . ha. No, friends don't use fine, right?
Right. But I know—we know—it's hard for you to
talk right now, but we love you, so we'll be here.
Standing creepily under your window until you're
ready to talk. Promise. None of this is your fault.

"But it feels like it."

I closed out of the screen, cutting her off.

I took a different route to the hospital that morning,
down a different street. A street I knew to be dangerous.
I felt the pulse beating at the back of my head and for a
moment when I stepped out into the road, I envisioned
the silence that would follow before the bile rushed up my
mouth and a horn blasted me back into the present.

I jumped back onto the sidewalk, embarrassed and
angry. I turned, going home. I didn't deserve to go to the
hospital today. I didn't deserve to see Annalise. I crawled
into my bed, shoes and everything, and slept through the
night.

THE NEXT MORNING I felt sick. The smell of butter on toast
made me want to puke. I grabbed an old apple, pocked
with brown spots, and stuffed it in my backpack. I didn't

notice Adam sitting at the kitchen table until I turned to leave.

"Where are you going?" His voice was barely above a whisper.

"Hospital."

Adam's back stiffened, and I dared him to say anything else as I walked out the back door. I was getting really good at sitting in the waiting area, letting the buzzing of the fluorescent lights above me turn into a sort of melody. I picked up a magazine, leafing through, never really looking at the pages. There was a puzzle at the back, but someone had already completed it. *Jerk*.

I didn't notice Annalise's mother as she slipped in and stood in front of me. She reached for the magazine, tugging it away from me. Placing her hand under my chin, she forced me to meet her eyes. "Back again?"

"Yes."

She pursed her lips, crossing her arms over her chest. "Annalise is asleep now. You'll have to come back later."

"I can see her?"

Mrs. Baker's answer was slow, deliberate. "Maybe. That's up to her. Or so she tells me."

"I'll wait for maybe."

She deflated just a bit, falling into the seat next to me. I took a moment to really observe, every part of her worn and drawn. Again I doubted myself. Why was I here? Why did I keep coming back? She caught me looking, and I turned away, embarrassed. I was useless and probably getting in the way, but now that I was here there must be something I could do. I pulled the apple from my bag, offering it up.

She shook her head, leaning back on the chair and closing her eyes. "That apple looks more tired than I am."

We didn't say much for a while, just sat and waited.

"It's Julia or Julie, isn't it?"

I nodded.

"Why do you come here, Julia?"

I shook my head. "I don't know."

Which was true. I had no idea why I came. Why I wanted to see Annalise. Did I want forgiveness? Should I be forgiven? Should I be blamed?

Her stomach made a rumbling sound, and I offered the apple once again. She took a bite, small, tentative, then turned to me. "I'm afraid it's no good."

The apple went in the trash, and Annalise's mother walked out the door.

MY LIFE AT home had become a silent film. My parents and I shuffled around each other, not saying a word. Adam kept to his room. Annalise's parents hadn't pressed charges, not yet, but the police were investigating and everything was a jumbled mess of legal terms that I didn't understand and couldn't follow. My parents spoke to our attorney, and I was advised not to visit the hospital anymore.

I did not follow their advice.

"Why do you go?"

Adam caught me leaving the house the next day, a fresh apple tucked in my bag.

"Why don't you?"

"I can't leave the house, you know that."

"Would you go if you could?"

He didn't answer right away. "I don't think I could look at her."

"Why not?"

Adam curled his arms around himself, trying to pull the words out but they were unwilling to come. I sat down, reached for his hand, hoping he would let me hold it. His arm would not budge, and he let mine rest on top of his.

"What happened that night?"

"You know what happened."

"I know what they say. What they keep talking about on the news, but I don't know, what you saw, what you did . . . I don't know how you didn't see her."

Adam shuddered. "I did see her."

I made my brain stop. Told it to wait for him to continue, knowing there was more to the story.

"After I peeled off I was angry, so damn angry, figured I should keep driving until it wore off, figured it was safest. I can't even remember how far I got; after a while it was just a lot of darkness and quiet. I felt heavy, pulled down, my eyes closing." He paused, wiping the tears at the corners of his eyes. "Then, then it was too late and I felt like

I was wading through, trying to wake up and move faster. I needed to move faster, and she was there and then she wasn't. It felt like forever before the car stopped, before I reached the pedal, before I got out of the car."

Adam's whole body was shaking. Small tremors that grew and grew until he broke, sobs tearing through him. "She was there, and I wouldn't go near her. I just kept staring like it was all a dream—it felt like a dream. Everything was hazy and out of focus. I tried thinking, in my head, wake up, wake up, time to wake up. But she didn't move. She didn't move. She would've moved if it was a dream, right? Right?"

"Yeah." I came around the table behind Adam and wrapped my arms around him. I pressed my face into his neck, whispering, "Then you called 911, Adam. You called 911."

"It took me too long. The numbers kept bouncing around in my head. I couldn't, couldn't find them."

We'd gotten the report from the police. Adam held Annalise's hand until they took her away and brought him to the station.

I held Adam until he stopped shaking and relaxed against me.

IN THE MORNING I sat down in my favorite waiting room chair, two apples in my bag that day. I sat and waited. When my heart threatened to leap out of my chest, I exited the room and went looking for Annalise. She wasn't hard to find—there was a large monitor near the nurses' station listing all the patients' last names. I watched her mother from across the hall arranging the many bouquets on the tiny table in Annalise's room. There was one bouquet of sunflowers. Annalise gestured for her mom to shift that one closer to her.

In that moment, watching her and her mother talk and laugh, I knew how wrong it was that I was here, that I had come looking for something to make myself feel better, because wasn't that the reason? I wanted to know that Annalise was all right so I could feel better about Adam. So Adam could feel better. I pivoted and was halfway down the hall when her mom's voice called me back.

"Leaving then?"

It felt like forever before I turned.

"Yeah."

Her mom leaned outside the door, and it clicked shut behind her. It didn't escape my notice that she was blocking my way to her daughter. I did not blame her. "She's doing better."

"Is she?"

"As much as she can be." She offered no more. I deserve no more.

"Right." Time slowed, it crawled, it dragged on until I thought of scratching my own skin off. "I'm sorry," I said, wondering how that word could mean so much and so little at the same time.

"I know you are."

I felt the tears prick at my eyes. "I know that doesn't help, but I am sorry."

"It might," she replied, coming closer. "Eventually."

Eventually.

"Those for me?" she motioned to the lumps in my bag. I pulled out the two apples and handed them to her. She brought them close to her nose, sniffing and nodded. "Much better today. I might actually eat them."

With a ghost of a smile—the first she'd given me, it felt like a blessing—she turned and left me in the hall.

THAT EVENING I spoke to my parents about leaving, about doing something outside our house. I didn't tell them about walking into the street, or going to the hospital. I simply told them I needed to leave, and they understood because they wanted to as well.

With a Little Help from Our Friends

JULIUS LESTER JAMES IS AN ANGEL. I TELL HIM THIS, AND HE laughs. "Please tell my husband that," he says as he pulls up on his Vespa. We are outlaws now, which is not true but it feels like it. I wasn't formally discharged but no one put up a fight when I limped out of the hospital—there was far too much going on for that. I promised Julius I'd return once I found Miles. I make it three blocks on my own, wheezing, limping, and tripping over pieces of New Orleans the hurricane had dumped on the streets. I was certain that it would take me a year before I reached our meet-up spot when I heard the *putt, putt, putt* of Julius's Vespa down the street. The mint-colored scooter brought tears to my eyes as it stopped in front of me.

"Now I hope you didn't think I was going to just let you walk all the way to Jackson Square in your condition?" Julius pats the seat behind him, scooting farther up to give me more space. He hands me a second helmet, and I hop on.

"I'm telling you, you are a guardian angel. I know it."

Julius laughs and waits for me to settle behind him. I'm getting mud and dirt all over the paint—the only clean parts of me are the borrowed shoes Julius begged from a nurse.

"I know. No one believes me when I tell them, though."

I wrap my arms around Julius's waist, and we take off through the streets, winding around broken glass and the crisscrossing cars moved by wind and water like pieces on a chessboard. The storm ripped signs from stores and relocated them blocks away. The New Orleans I'd walked through hours ago has been rearranged as if shaken in a globe, its details scattered across different streets and roads. My stomach lurches with the constant jostling. I hide my face in Julius's neck.

"Take a breath now, we're almost there."

I nod, concentrating on the sound of the Vespa, the feel of the wind—actually pleasant now and not at all trying to kill me. But with block after block of bumps and swerves to avoid fallen branches I need something else to focus on. "How long have you and your husband been together?"

"Twenty years."

"That's amazing."

"It's not bad." He turns back with a smile.

"How did you meet?"

"Oh—the old cliché. Handsome doctor meets strapping young nurse followed by a tryst here and a stolen kiss there in between shifts. Both of us pretending it was just that, of course."

"Of course." I smile, my first real one since last night.

Julius's voice vibrates with memories of love. It travels all the way back to me, soothing and assured, making me wish I was holding onto Miles as I listen to his story. "Then before we knew it, we'd become each other's lives. He has his flaws, of course, but I get by; I'm an angel like that."

"Flaws?" I know a setup when I hear one.

"Man likes plain vanilla ice cream. Who likes plain vanilla? And with nothing on it too. Crazy, right? Everyone knows mint chocolate chip is the only perfect flavor."

JACKSON SQUARE IS empty when we arrive—ravaged. Fences have been pulled up by the roots, bent and twisted. Piles and piles of torn newspapers and garbage lie against the cathedral entrance like gathered leaves in the fall. Julius helps me off the scooter, guiding me as far as we can go. I scream for Miles over and over again, but there's no answer.

"Where is everyone?"

"Hopefully far away from here." Julius leads me back to the Vespa. "We got at least twenty injured this morning.

Less than we prepared for, so thank goodness for tiny miracles. I guess some people do learn." He helps me back onto the bike. "Keep going, Julia, keep going. Don't give up now."

ON WE GO. Sometimes the shoreline is the easiest way, the water washing everything with it until we hit a patch of cars acting like a barricade; then it's a right and a left down narrow streets that aren't covered with sprinkled branches and garbage. My eyes water from the wind blowing across my face—at least that's what I tell myself. "Thank you for doing this, Julius." My voice is a whisper. "You didn't—"

He waves it off. "Maybe I need a happy ending to this day too."

A happy ending. Will we be so lucky? Julius and I head to Miles's favorite place by the river. A moment of panic sets in because I don't recognize it at first. The storm has relocated street signs and a few of the lamps have fallen over. I almost can't find the spot where his bracelet fell through the planks of the pier. Once again I thank God for Julius, who knows which street is which by heart no matter how much it's all changed.

"Damn." Julius voice is constrained; when I look back he's shaking his head as he surveys the damage. "Damn. All the hard work cleaning this city up, and here comes Dorothy barreling down on us."

"Dorothy? Really?"

"Ain't it cheeky? Bet someone thought it was funny."
He shakes his head. "Wish the world would stop knocking
us down."

I am not graceful getting off the Vespa again.

"Still, not as bad as Katrina. That's something. We
would've needed a kayak to make our way through the
Quarter."

"You were here during Katrina?"

"I was." He wags his finger at me. "Don't tell anyone
I was that stupid. I stayed behind to help a friend and got
stuck. Yeah, that was bad. Whole sides of buildings falling
off, houses just . . . just gone. Torn apart like toys. Dorothy did her best"—he turns away from me—"and it will
take us time to pull ourselves up, but she has nothing on
Katrina. We're still coming back from that one."

I get as close to the shore as I can, scanning the waters,
which were not very clear before Dorothy and are even less
so now.

Julius stands by me. "You weren't hoping to find him *in*
the water, were you?"

"I don't know. We were out of the water, we were . . ."
But what if he was pulled back in? We were still too close
to the river, it would've been so easy to slip. "I'm hoping to
find him anywhere. Alive."

But he wasn't at the hospital. And they had no record
of him as a patient. Which didn't mean anything, I told
myself. Maybe he wasn't as injured? Maybe . . . Had

someone taken me here and left him behind? Maybe he was holed up somewhere, waiting. Image after image flashes through my mind: Miles dragged back into the water. Or lying in a hospital bed unconscious. No ID, no name . . . Miles leaving me on a bed, saying good-bye. We spent one night together; he didn't owe me being there. I curve into myself, concentrating on the pain. I would accept being angry, being abandoned, being one night among many, if it meant he is still alive.

Liar, my heart says, and it is a little bit right.

"Anything?"

I stand, lungs trying their best to take in air.

"Take it easy, Miss Julia." He steadies me. "You got hit by something big. Left you bruised."

I lift my shirt, examining my belly again. I'd been too scared to look down at the hospital. Blue and purple blossoms across my side and down my stomach—a Rorschach of injuries; I take a good look, finding tiny cuts and scratches dotting my skin. There are more that I can't see, but I can feel them—they call to me, keep me awake, keep me moving. They sing along my back, catching on the fabric of my shirt, and along my legs. My bandaged wrist throbs, and I turn it a bit, testing its limits.

I survived. I will keep going. I will keep looking. "One more place?"

Julius pulls out his phone, checks it, and nods. "I can make time for that."

• • •

GLITTER ENDURES LIKE cockroaches—even after the storm there are still remnants of it along the streets; it makes the piles of debris gathered along the gutter shine. The avenues of Carrollton are filled with life, though a stark difference to the beats of Mid-Summer. Those that stayed behind have already started to clear the dead branches and broken glass, making our journey a bit easier. We travel down the parade route, keeping my eyes open for Miles. Even after the storm I recognize the streets we traveled down, my mind replaying the fun, the laughter, the vibrancy. We continue on, and my eyes shift to the rooftop where the best amateur production of *Romeo and Juliet* happened. It doesn't look like there was any major damage, though the hanging sign for the shop below is no longer there; we find it two blocks down.

Still no Miles. A hollowness descends; maybe I should be back at the hospital, waiting for my parents, healing.

"Maybe we should go back?"

"You sure?" Julius replies.

"No, not at all."

We loop around and make it halfway out of the neighborhood before I spot him.

"STOP!" I shout. When the Vespa stops, each injury sparks to life as I jump off the back.

"Sunshine?"

It's not the voice I want to hear, and it doesn't sound

the same coming from Taj's lips, but the name still brings a little soul back into me. Before I know it I'm being pulled off my feet into Taj's arms, choking back a sob.

"I knew we made a connection." He steps back with a sly grin on his face.

I laugh, wiping away the tears.

Julius comes up. "This your boy?"

I shake my head. "This is a friend of his. Taj, this is Julius, my angel."

"Pleasure." Taj and Julius shake hands. "Hope you have some miracles left for this neighborhood." Taj turns back to me. "Why are you here? Is Miles with you?"

My face falls, all the happiness I felt from seeing a familiar face wiped away.

"What happened?"

"We got separated." I straighten, trying to summon more strength than I have. I think I ran out of adrenaline back at the river and all I have left is stubbornness. "At the river."

His eyes grow wide before he presses his hand against his temple. "I haven't seen him," Taj replies. "I was going to check on Danny next. We lost contact after the tail hit. Hoping he heard from D too."

"Domínguez? Right."

"I haven't heard from him since he left with that girl from the party. Not that any calls are going through. I got some texts through earlier, but no responses yet."

Julius taps me on the shoulder. "Sorry to interrupt,

Julia, but I need to head back to the hospital."

"I'm staying," I reply in my firmest voice, giving him a quick hug. "I'll be okay."

He looks me up and down, then over to Taj before deciding. "Take my phone."

"No, it's fine."

"Take my phone—there wasn't one among your stuff so I know you don't have one. Maybe eventually you'll be able to get a call through." Julius shoves his cell phone into my hand. "Hospital's number is on there. Eddie's number—that's my husband—is on there as well. He'll find me. Promise me you'll call me if you need me, Miss Julia."

"Promise."

His eyes narrow. "Why do I know you are lying?"

"I'm not lying. I will call if I need you, Julius."

He hesitates but has no choice and hugs me again, a gentle good-bye. I can almost feel him pouring more energy into me, knowing that I'll need it later. "I expect you back at the hospital before this day is done."

"I promise." And I do. Deep down I know I only have this one day to find Miles, probably less, before they take me home and I've lost him for good.

I watch Julius ride off until I can no longer see him.

"You make friends fast, Julia," Taj says behind me. Funny to think that Taj knows my name before Miles did. Before Miles will.

"I do?" I don't know if Julius would consider me a

friend, but he has been a friend to me. I think of him returning to work, to the person he loves, and my heart lightens. That means something.

"I'm going to check on Danny." Taj motions for me to follow but I reach for his hand.

"I'm not going."

"What?"

"I need to keep looking, and I can't slow down." I hand over Julius's phone.

"You saying I'm slow?"

"Yes. I need to find Miles and you need to find Danny. Put your number in the phone. I find him or you find him, we'll text each other, okay?"

Taj hesitates, and I reach over to take it back. I don't have time for this.

"Okay, okay." He holds the phone away from me as a man with a strong resemblance to him catches up. He nods and watches the interaction. Taj hands the phone back.

"You better text me when you find him," he says.

"Ditto."

I'm halfway down the street when I hear Taj yell, "Yo! You might need his real name, right? It's—"

Taj is drowned out by a blaring car horn and all I hear is "Mills"—something Mills or Mills something, I have no idea.

"What?" I yell back, but Taj is waving, giving me a thumbs-up before he turns and leaves.

Of course. I would laugh if I had any humor left.

I continue on at a snail's pace, maneuvering around mountains of garbage that have been blown onto the street corners. Along the way I pick up a large stick that's just the right length for me to use as a cane. I pass a woman picking up broken shards of glass and wet photos off the street; the hurricane imploded her windows, sucking out all the picture frames from her walls.

"I forgot to take them down," she mumbles. "How could I forget to take them down?"

She is not the only one picking up pieces of her life that have been scattered to the wind. If I find any personal items I place them by the nearest house, knowing they'll find their way home somehow. It feels like the least I can do as I walk by on my own journey, not able to help more.

I make my way forward, fatigue now a close friend. As the day goes on, more and more people appear on their lawns. I ask the people around if they've seen Miles—Mills, I say and hope they know the name. I describe him from the tip of his blue hair down to his hole-ridden Chucks, hoping the details help. Some say they think they maybe saw him earlier but don't know where he went. My heart leaps each time. He's alive! He was here, he was just here. I curse my slow-moving body trailing just behind his.

And yet, my mind fills with doubt. Did they really see him? Or maybe they are confusing him with something else. Others didn't see him at all and hadn't seen him since the Midsummer Boys left after the parade. They don't have time for follow-up questions—they have their own people to find, their own lives to track down.

Down a block I catch a glimpse of blue hair and every inch of me sparks alive. I'm running, hobbling, down the street calling "Miles," moving people out of the way with my stick like a crazy person. "Miles!" I yell, but he doesn't turn. Maybe I'm not loud enough. Maybe he's forgotten the name I gave him and me along with it. Then I'm there, my hand reaching for his. "Miles."

I turn him toward me; it feels like my heart will burst through my rib cage.

But it's not him—I sag just as quickly, exhaustion taking over. I lean against the stick, dejected. This guy is too short and now that I look at his hair it is nowhere near electric blue. How could I have ever thought he was Miles?

"You okay, miss?"

I release his arm. "No. I'm sorry." I have no energy to lie.

"You better sit down then."

My body agrees, and I collapse on someone's front steps, taking a moment to collect myself. I will not give up, but I need this moment to settle, to plan my path. As I calculate where I need to go and how far I need to travel, I scan the people in the neighborhood. Those that stuck around exit their homes to survey the damage and help neighbors with theirs as well. Piles of branches, trash, and broken glass are ushered to the edges of the streets. If the storm hadn't hit us they would be piling empty cups, discarded clothing, and costumes. Little by little the hurricane's effects are bundled together and tossed out.

I can't shake the shivers running up my spine—something is off, more than just broken glass and beaten-up streets. It's the music, or lack thereof. In its place the sounds of hundreds of insects build to a pitch, a static that is far too familiar. New Orleans should never sound like this.

Around me, people pull sheets of wood off their windows, and I think of the storeowner I met last night and wonder how she fared. I add her shop to the list of places to visit.

I check Julius's cell phone, but there have been no messages. I text Taj:

Anything?

It takes five minutes before it goes through. The reply comes ten minutes later.

Nothing. His family hasn't heard from him either.

I shove the phone back in my pocket. Decision time. I'm going to retrace my steps, no matter how long it takes. Starting with the Mid-Summer route, ending at the pier. If I don't . . . if I don't find him then, then I'll head back to Jackson Square and then . . . then I don't know, wait, I guess. Wait for him to find me or for my parents to arrive. Call Taj, check hospitals; there have to be missing persons lines for emergencies, right? I exhale, already annoyed at my own plan, but I'm sticking with it. The memories from last night map out my route: the parade, the Maple Leaf, the rooftop . . . I head out toward my first stop when a hand grabs my shoulder, turning me around.

For one brief moment my heart believes it will be Miles. Ever the optimist.

The Multi-State Traveler

"JULIE."

I push the hand away, fighting a wave of repulsion. Tavis.

"How the hell did you find me? GPS?"

"Julie, this is stupid." He's reaching for me, trying to pull me into his arms. "You're going to hurt yourself."

"Go away, Tavis." I hobble away from him, looking up at the sky as I do. *If this is some sort of test having to do with patience, God, I'm fine with failing it.*

"I'm not going to leave you, Julie." He matches my pace, which isn't hard to do at the moment. "You're acting insane."

"Then you should probably stay far, far away from me," I say as I demonstrate how to do so.

"I promised your brother I would take care of you."

"How dare you act like you were ever even friends!" I whirl to face him, ready to jab him with my stick. "I happen to know Adam hasn't spoken to anyone since—since—just go away!"

Tavis puts his hands up. "Fine, but I'm in charge of this trip and responsible for you . . . and . . . I care for you."

We are making a scene; people stare as I continue on.

"Good for you." I keep going, Tavis at my heels, like I owe him something. As if saying he likes me entitles him to whatever he happens to want. He's faster than me with my broken toe and swollen ankle. He comes around, blocking my way, trying to take my hand. I do not have time for this. "Please move."

"Not until you listen." He rests a hand on my arms, trying to calm me down. Trying to restrain me. No thank you. I pull my arms away, almost losing my balance in the process.

"I care for you, Julie," he says. "I always have."

I don't think I've ever laughed in a mocking manner before now, but it just comes out. "Always." I have a very hard time believing anything Tavis says.

"There is no always, Tavis. We didn't speak until I came here—before then you were just some guy in my school and at church. That's it. Proximity does not make a relationship. Take. The. Hint."

Tavis shakes his head, an impressive amount of denial

happening right now. "I know you think you don't have feelings for me, that you think of me only as a friend."

I am shaking with anger, my heart hammering against my chest, my face is red. I have to find Miles. Why does he not understand that he's holding me back?

"Let me stop you there—I don't think of you at all."

"That's a lie."

"Okay, fine. I do—" But not in that way. I'm about to say, *I think of you in the "isn't he so annoying" way,* when Tavis interrupts with "I knew it!" and grabs me, pulling me to him, sharp jabs of pain jutting through my body, my cries stifled by his lips crashing into mine.

His kiss is wet, cold, utterly mechanical, and, oh yeah, unwanted. He kisses me for a second or however long it takes my hand to push him away. I swat him with the stick and use it to wrench myself from his grasp. I fight the urge to wipe my mouth, then decide I don't care if it offends him. "Don't you ever do that again."

"You're not as strong as you think you are, Jules."

I block his next attempt, straight up shoving the stick in his chest.

"And you don't have to be; it's okay to show me you're hurting. I'm here now. I'm here." Tavis reaches for a strand of my hair. I can see how this is playing in his head, the romantic kiss, followed by the sweet pushing of the hair behind the ear. Ugh. I don't have time for this.

"No touching."

I swat his hand away, but the stupid smile on his lips is harder to get rid of. He looks me up and down, like he's "won" me—I mentally punch him in the face.

He moves to cup my cheek, and I shift. Panic rises—I'm losing valuable time standing here. This needs to end.

"One more time—" My words catch in midsentence, eyes darting to the shiny item on Tavis's wrist like a magpie. "What's this?" I grab his arm hard; he tries to pull away, to hide his wrist, but it's too late. I've seen it. Fury engulfs me, and I turn into a friggin' banshee, forcing Tavis against a wall, tugging at his hand until I'm able to remove the bracelet. Its patchwork self feels so light on the palm of my hand. It's a gift having it back, a sign. I tuck it in my pocket for safekeeping.

"Julie, I—"

"How did you get this?" In a rage, I press my arm on Tavis's neck and lean in. "The truth. Now."

"I don't—"

"NOW." I lean in, pressing harder with my arm, until I notice he can't speak so I let him go.

"I thought if you saw it, it would upset you."

I shake my head, no time for excuses.

"You're far too vulnerable right now, and something like this, a boy like that? He'll only hurt you. Trust me, it wasn't what you needed."

I think of leaning into Tavis's injured arm, of causing him pain until he talks, but I don't need to. Tavis is not strong, not like Abuela Julia, not like Miles, and not like me. Tavis caves.

"What I need?" My voice is low. "How would you know what I need?"

"Julie, please."

My fingers dig into the wood as I hold myself steady. "Just tell me what happened."

"I wasn't there when he brought you in, I swear."

Miles. Miles brought me in? My heart leaps. I nod. "And?"

"He saw me later, after they fixed you up and you were resting."

"He stayed?"

"For a bit."

He stayed.

"Why didn't he check in? How did he find you?"

"I don't know. I was in the waiting room; they'd bandaged me up and he recognized me from Mid-Summer. Asked me—asked me to look after you. Said he had to go check on his friends and family or something."

He left me, my heart whispers even as my brain points out the logic. *You were safe.*

But he left me, my heart repeats.

"And the bracelet?"

"He—he put it on you before he left so you'd know he'd been there." He tries to straighten, but I push him against the wall. "So you'd know he'd come back."

"And you took it."

"For safekeeping," he replies, completely sincere. He truly believes he's doing the right thing. "There's a lot of looting that happens after a disaster, Julie. You can't trust anyone."

That's hilarious coming from him. "Then?"

"Then he left you, Julie. He dropped you off. And don't get me wrong, I thank God he did, but he left. He didn't stay with you. I stayed. I sat by your side and waited till you woke up. I called your parents."

"You called my parents?"

"Of course I did. Your father is coming to get you as soon as they open the airports."

I brush my fingers along the bracelet one more time. The feel bringing me back to Miles, to our night, curled into him, playing poker, kissing, touching.

"I know this kind of guy, Julie. He's not worth it. He's not going to be there for you. In the end there were more important things to him than you."

My heart stops, Tavis's comment wrenching me out of my memories. "That's not true."

"Isn't it?" He moves closer. "I'm not judging you, but you were just one night, Julie, and that night is over."

Yes, absolutely, family is important to Miles. His friends are important. But he hadn't been at home, hadn't been at Danny's or Taj's—had he? Where did he go? Where is he now? For a moment I think Tavis might be right. Miles left me. There were more important things. It was just one night.

My fingers reach for the bracelet again; image after image flickers through my mind. Miles at Mid-Summer, Miles in the pool, holding my hand, Miles curled around me as I slept, then standing naked as a jaybird, Miles giving me the bracelet his grandfather made, Miles diving in to pull me out of the river, holding me against the current, his voice echoing even after the darkness took its hold. Then another image, one most likely created by my own mind, but I embrace it nonetheless—Miles pulling me out, carrying me, waiting for me somewhere.

All that is worth so much.

"I don't care," I say, dropping my arm and walking away from Tavis. "Still going to find him."

"You've got to be kidding me. Please, Julie, just forget this guy. Come back with me. He's already forgotten you, I promise."

I take a deep breath. "Go fuck yourself, Tavis, from the bottom of my heart."

"Julie—"

"Don't try to follow me—I will knee you in the groin. Or I'll press robbery charges."

"Robbery?"

I point to the bracelet. "This was given to me as a gift, and you took it. You stole it as far as I'm concerned. So don't follow me or once again I will press charges."

Surprisingly, Tavis actually listens as I leave him behind, my anger carrying me down several blocks before I notice how far I've gone. It doesn't hollow me out this time; I touch the bracelet on my wrist and feel renewed. I forge on, unsure how long this energy will last. When I'm halfway out of Carrollton I stop, and the pain catches up to me. I was apparently on painkillers. And now each twinge, each pang is amplified, it echoes. My teeth clench when I lean against a broken post, its metallic whine a mirror of my own pain. As I walk on the people of Carrollton call out: *You okay there, hon? Easy now, girl. Okay, sweetheart?*

The Maple Leaf is no luck, but the kind people clearing out the space offer me a glass of water before I continue on. I leave them Julius's number, and they promise to call if they see him. Miles, I say, that's what I call him, I explain, but it's not his real name, no, I don't know his real name, something Mills, I think. Just please, if you see him.

I am warmed. I am hopeful. I am aided by the people of New Orleans. When I think I can't continue I watch them pick up the broken bits of their city, moving forward even through the pain. So I move. I help and they help. They offer rides, offer to walk with me, as I make my way to Loyola Cathedral, Café Du Monde, and back to Jackson Square. They bless me. They wish me luck. Some know the Mills boy, some thought they saw him, yeah sure, 'bout an hour ago, maybe two? He went this way or that? It no longer bothers me that their answers are not concrete. I pass by the club we danced in, and it is the worst I've seen so far. Half of the roof has collapsed, and people hover around the outside.

"What happened?" I ask the nearest person to me.

"Roof was rotten through. Owner never did fix it and, well, I guess it didn't survive the storm."

"Did anyone get hurt?"

"Don't know, kid. Still trying to get them out." He walks away and toward the building. All those people. The tears are pouring down my cheeks. I let them. I hope they decided to go home after all.

"Where's the ambulance?" I shout back to the man. He looks up and shrugs.

I try calling 911, but nobody picks up. I heard in some states you can actually text 911, so I give it a try. It goes through but there's no response. I text Julius's husband about it as well. Then I text Taj.

I feel bad leaving, but I'm no use to anyone—I can't lift anything heavy and I'm just standing in their way. I decide to head out, calling 911 one more time on my way. It goes through, and I give them the address.

I make it to the shop where we bought our supplies, happy to see the boards held through the night.

I check in with Taj again—the text doesn't go through. I'll try later.

I hitch a ride to the hotel with an older woman heading out to check on her sister. At the hotel, the damage is surface mostly, with broken windows being the worst of it. We'd locked the hotel before we left, and now the door won't budge. Neither does the one in back. I drag over a trash can, using it to see over the fence, and the once-peaceful luminescent bay we'd played in is gone, filled with garbage, making it as opaque as the Mississippi. My voice is hoarse. I call out Miles's name. People watch me; they let me pass; they nod as I go—a silent wish for luck. They have their own names to call out too.

I wind down, body ticking, flame fading bit by bit. Though the sky is still a dull gray, it is beyond humid and I am as soaked as I was after the rain last night.

I make my way over to the pier where Miles and I saw each other last. This is where I stop, where the flame sputters and my legs give.

This is good, this is where I'll stay, I think. *Forever or for a little bit.* Blocks away a group of men start shouting. I watch, my head throbbing—two of them look like Miles. I rub my eyes, tired of their deception. The argument breaks up. I go back to staring at the ground, imagining hours passing by with each blink. Maybe I'll click my heels three times and my body will be magically transported. *But,* I sigh, *that wouldn't make me happy either.*

My eyes close, I slack, stars float up, just beyond reach. A cool breeze comes along, a remnant of Dorothy, and more welcome than its predecessor.

"It's okay." I hear Abuela Julia's voice. I imagine her

sitting next to me. "It's okay to take a moment. It does not mean you are giving up, *niña*. We all need time, *un momento* to gather, to rest, even to think all hope is lost. Yes, even that. Be lost. Be sad. Be. Y *cuando estes lista, respira*. And you will find the agony bearable, enough to stand. *Te lo prometo*."

The stars disappear as my eyes open, and Abuela Julia fades away. I wipe the tears and test my body, wiggling my fingers and touching bruises. The pain is still there, but so am I.

"Fairy Girl."

This is nice, I think. A dream, a waking dream . . . I don't care. I want to wrap myself around the sound of his voice.

"Red-Winged Fairy Girl."

I smile. Keep going, I need more. I conjure up the sounds of Mid-Summer. The trumpets, the drums, the laughter. They swell around me, bringing with them the dances along the streets, delicious treats and shared stories, his lips against mine . . . especially his lips against mine. I welcome it all back.

A shadow falls in front of me, long and lean. Followed by a hand on my shoulder. "Well, you're a tough one. How about Sunshine?"

A hand below my chin, pulling my face up. A smile. Electric. The sun is not in its full glory, but it's bright enough that the blue in his hair blasts through the fog in my mind.

Curse you, brain, for being so slow, so unbelieving. That line connecting those dots at a snail's pace. Not understanding, not trusting, not even when he's right here, kneeling down, hand on my cheek. I blink. I tear up. He wipes them away—his touch—it's real. My brain is finally coming to. *You can stop now, Julie, you found him.*

He wraps himself around me, and I wrap myself around him, his breath on my neck, his hands along my back. We are both battered. We are both damaged. And still, we stand.

"Julie," I say. "My name is Julia Marie Eagan Hostos . . . or just Julie."

"Much better than Lila." He pulls away far enough to take a good look at me. "You think I can finally get your number?"

I kiss him, pulling him down for our lips to reach. Our mouths part. He kisses me like he would take me in, to consume, to remember, to hold on to forever. I let him.

The bracelet stays with me, a reminder and a promise. I run my fingers across the face of its gold plate, feeling for his birth date on one side and then the newly discovered second etching across the other side: his name. *In front of me the whole time.* I trace the calligraphy with my thumb, feel the name out on my tongue. *Jeremiah Mills.* It fits him, it fits us.

We stay in each other's arms.

This is the beginning. We both know, no matter what we are or what we will be, this is just the start. The spark.

I kiss him again. I smile against his lips, knowing no one else will kiss him like I have. Around us the music picks up, even if it's only in my own head.

I kiss him, and it tastes like sunshine.

Acknowledgments

ONE HUNDRED THANK-YOUS to Maria Barbo, my fantastic editor, for inviting me to be part of this journey and for being there every step of the way. You are a truly fantastic champion and motivator. You've made this quite a lovely experience.

To my family and friends, for all the support through the years, for asking questions and constantly wondering when this book would come out—thank you for the mild anxiety, and here it is! Please don't ask when the next one is coming—I'm working on it.

To the rest of my kick-ass Harper team that already rules the school: My publicist, Rosanne "Ro" Romanello, fate keeps bringing us together, girl, it is meant to be!

Future killer senior editors Kelsey Horton and Rebecca Schwarz, thank you for falling in love with Miles as well. Alexei Esikoff, my production editor, Jean McGinley in subrights, and Alana Whitman and Carmen Alvarez in the marketing team for all that you do for this book. A big hug to Katie Fitch and Amy Ryan in the art department for the gorgeous cover.

And thank you to you, the reader, for investing in this story. It's a cliché to say I wouldn't be here without you, but it is true.

Pinky swear.

8-11-16

2-9-22 1-9-20

6(any) 5

1 1